Tab Ends

A collection of thematically jarring short stories.

By

Ants Ambridge.

Also, by the same Author;

The Night Out

Backbones

GY 'til I Die

Under the Unfamiliar Moon

Available in paperback and on Kindle through
Amazon.

For my family.

The Bottomless Pond.

At the end of the road 'Suggitt's Lane' in Cleethorpes, is a large pond. The rumour for many years stated it stood bottomless. Now regardless of which shape you think the earth is, this was quite obviously bollocks. Others speculated that it went incredibly deep and fed into most major waterways and seas in and around the UK. One person claimed to have spotted Nessie in it.

Known as Chapman's Pond, the rumours continued year after year. Some claimed the Viking Grim's original secret treasure remained hidden in an alcove. Others claim that a drunken bus driver once lost an entire double decker in it, the vehicle form, not the chocolate bar. One local man decided two things a few years ago. The first thing he decided; he was a scientist, despite having no qualifications whatsoever, not even a GSCE pass. The second thing was that he would permanently put an end to the myths for good. So, begins the tale of Tim Bikkelmurr.

Tim did rigorous preparation for almost three days beforehand. By preparation, this meant he rented a wetsuit and spent the rest of the time drinking in the Swashbuckle Tavern telling everyone that caught his eye he was a scientist and going to prove what no-one previously had been able to. As his day arrived, he expected a jubilant throng to witness his discovery, but grew disappointed to see not a soul. He waited a while.

He'd changed into the rented wetsuit, which fit too snugly in some parts, specifically his understated beer belly, and hung too loose in others. To make it airtight, he had taped the wrists and ankles to his flesh. It was April, so still seasonably cold; he didn't relish the idea of jumping in immediately. To pass the time, until hopefully it warmed up, he slung debris into the pond–rocks, stones, mud, stray cats etc. Hours passed by and he realised that no one would show up, and it wouldn't get any hotter, he decided to take the plunge.

After visiting the shops and eliciting a few funny looks for being in a wetsuit, he emerged with a bottle of whiskey in hand and took a few healthy belts from it. If the outside of his body was to be cold, he would warm it from within. He strode with a determined gait to the broken piece of fencing that allowed him access to the pond.

Tim placed his snorkel into his mouth, he took a running jump into the pond. "Bastard!" he gasped as his head re-emerged, snorkel wrapped around the back of his head. He had forgotten to put his flippers on. He needed them, he guessed. Tim splashed towards the shore to put them on. Shivering, he also finished the whiskey to brave a second jump into the murky waters.

The second time, his running jump took a turn for the worse as he tripped over the flippers, tumbling in from the side. As he frantically doggy paddled to a shallower portion of the pond, he rearranged his goggles and snorkel, so they provided a use for him. He dove underwater.

Disappointed, he soon reached the bottom of the pond. He tried again and again from different spots, but there was a clear finite space below the pond's surface. He looked for holes that possibly led to deeper parts. Tim found four shopping trolleys and a television, but no holes. He emerged and swam back to the bank to get out of the water and change. He couldn't believe no-one had done this before. Tim made the decision to report his findings as soon as possible.

Changing back into his clothes quickly, he almost jogged the entire way to the Swashbuckle Tavern.

Gregg, the barman rolled his eyes as Tim burst through the doors yelling, "I've done it! Guys! I solved the mystery of Chapman's Pond!" There sat only three other patrons in the pub, alcoholics all; a common sight most days of the week. They barely registered his presence, as even to committed piss artists as themselves, Tim was a pain in the arse. Usually he spent his days propping up the bar and complaining about bus routes in the area.

Tim continued, oblivious to the lack of interest shown by his only friends. "For years, nobody knew if Chapman's Pond had a bottom! Today, I can confirm it has! Pint of lager and double whiskey please." Gregg dutifully poured the drinks and requested payment. Tim's disappointment that his discovery didn't warrant even one free drink was clear on his face. Gregg shrugged in response to Tim's pleading eyes. "I don't get one on the house for proving the unprovable?"

Under normal circumstances, Gregg would bite his tongue; as annoying as the customers were, they remained customers after all. Most importantly, ones that drank throughout the day, thus warranting the hours Gregg desperately needed to work. Something about Tim always bugged Gregg more than most, perhaps the way he seemed to believe he was 'above' everyone else, despite his loser nature. "You know that's a kid's story, right?" Tim looked at Gregg with menace as he continued, "I mean, there was a massive flagpole sticking out of it for ages too. Kind of proves that 'science' already knew it had a bottom".

Tim pouted. He felt deflated, but Gregg had not finished, "So you swam to the bottom, did you?" Tim nodded and added, "With a wetsuit and snorkel". Gregg smirked, "So you must be well enough to look for work again then?" The other patrons laughed at this exchange, to which Tim glowered and turned to take a seat close to the window.

As he gazed across the waters of the Humber, he squinted and saw either Hull or Spurn Point in the distance. "I reckon I could swim that" he thought to himself.

A Christmas in the UK

He warmed his hands on the fire. It'd already been a cold winter and now was only early December. The flat he lived in appeared barren. His living room contained a TV, the last remnants of his previous life, and a worn sofa, provided by a charity. On that sofa he lay curled up, screwing his nose in distaste at the faint tobacco smells that it still emitted, despite the amount of fabric freshener he'd previously used on it.

He pulled the blanket further around himself. He sensed the warmth in the room rising, which felt comforting. The TV showed an inane reality show in the background. He paid no attention to the relentless bellowing of the hateful protagonists. He contemplated changing the channel, but it would be the same story on them all, he guessed. His entertainment no longer entertained him. The thin, white curtains that remained in the flat when he moved in blew slightly from the draughts on multiple parts of the window. He hated those curtains; useless pieces of shit. They blocked no light in the summer and flapped constantly from the wind in winter.

Gaps through the curtains revealed the street outside, rows of houses seemingly trying to outdo each other with how gaudy a spectacle they made with their Christmas decorations. He quite simply couldn't afford to put up even a sprig of mistletoe this year, not that he would as he no longer held a reason to celebrate. There would be no turkey at Christmas for him this year, nor any family to share it with, not since he left his wife, leaving the kids with her. She'd protested, but he'd become a millstone around their necks dragging them down and he'd no ability to provide for them.

Three years previously, it'd been different. Christmas proved a happy time. He would revel in the overjoyed smiles on his children's faces as they anticipated the big day itself. Their excitement grew over the weeks leading up as they put up decorations, proud that ones they had made at school would be displayed prominently. Christmas TV specials began, so he and his wife would allow them to stay up later than usual to watch as a family, occasionally allowing them small amounts of eggnog or mulled wine. When the day arrived, the products of him and his wife saving all year piled under the tree, lovingly wrapped with bows and cards. He considered himself to be lucky to have such grateful children as they thanked their parents after opening each gift, even the clothes.

They would enjoy their dinner and spend the afternoon playing games with the children. He had always made a point of buying them both a board game each that they would endeavour to play as much as possible. He'd witnessed so many other parents who would simply get their children a games console and allow them to shut themselves away almost permanently. Whilst he and their mother bought their kids the same consoles, it seemed that because they attempted to spend family time together, their actions were reciprocated often. He missed the family, but understood it would destroy them to see him as he was now.

Then came the heart attack; in his thirties, an unexpected blow. The family, devastated and panicked, stay with him as he recovered in hospital. Pride forced him to adopt a forced bravado for them, despite the creeping terror of mortality. The doctors informed him he would need to undergo multiple operations over the course of his life. He didn't even remember the name they gave his condition anymore, the medication he needed to take made his mind fuzzy and caused sporadic memory loss. The main thing that concerned him; he'd been told working would no longer be an option.

His wife worked too, and for a while, they'd struggled with her low wage and his illness benefits. Then a further obstacle came when he was declared 'fit for work' and they stopped his illness benefits, despite the words of his doctors and consultants. He launched an appeal in vain, but they simply stated that their assessment was correct and that he needed to claim a benefit for people looking for work. Because of his wife's income, he wasn't entitled to the benefit they'd pushed him to claim, so he frantically tried to gain some other kinds of work that wouldn't put the physical strain on his weakened and failing heart. Every interview he attended, which were seldom, he helplessly watched the job slip away as they asked why the previous employment ended and he responded honestly. They would smile and suggest they were 'sorry to hear about your condition' and he wouldn't hear from them again. He understood perfectly, why would they want to employ someone likely to be off for several months after a bout of heart surgery?

He became withdrawn and worse, began snapping at his family. His wife shouldered the burden of providing for him and the children on a minimum wage. Every time he would verbally lash out at them, guilt and shame would wash over him and he began despising himself. His heart disease had become a cancer for the family. He couldn't take hurting them anymore, so one day when they visited her relatives, he packed a few personal items, including his gaming TV and simply left. He applied for a grotty little flat that no-one else wanted through the council and moved his meagre possessions in.

His wife rang daily for a few months, cajoling, pleading, berating. She tried to get him to come back, but the sight of his family suffering because of his own mounting bitterness pained him too much. Every time she called, he considered caving in and trying to work it out, but he perceived no future for himself. He repeatedly told her to forget about him and move on. Then she stopped calling, which devastated him even more. It was easier to be away with the daily contact, which proved the highlight of any given day, despite the hurt it caused the both of them. He still loved her dearly.

The TV crackled, and the screen went black. The sides of the TV began to drip, melting plastic dripping to the hardwood floor with a fizzle. As he predicted, the hardwood fireplace

13

was a fire hazard and the flames from his overloading with parts from a broken chair had spread quickly. Parts of the floor where the plastic had melted on smouldered now. He turned and faced the back of the couch and curled up. He hoped his wife would know to sue the council for letting such a fire risk and by his passing, he'd provide adequately for the children, more than he would alive.

His back seared with the rising heat. He hoped the smoke inhalation took him before the flames.

Birds.

George pedalled furiously down the North Wall overlooking the Humber estuary. He did this almost daily in the summer. The sea breeze gusting in his face, whilst his chubby, white legs pumped a rhythm provided an adequate workout for George, who, by his own admission, was a lazy man.

He approached the docks and slowed his pace with trepidation. Seagulls. 'I fucking hate seagulls', he thought to himself angrily. Every day, the same thing happened, he would encounter the beady-eyed bastards; Squawking and diving for scraps of fish meal from the one factory left on the docks. It wasn't so much hatred of seagulls, but fear of birds in general that led to his irrational reaction.

Then it happened. With a splat, one gull defecated on his t-shirt, making it appear as if the skull emblazoned on it had been a participant in a bukkake.

-   You shit cunt!

George shouted at the departing bird ineffectually. Rage swept over him as he plotted his revenge.

After arriving home, he ordered a gas-powered BB gun from Amazon. His plan would take between 4-5 days to come to fruition. It would have been less, but he couldn't afford Prime.

The gun arrived the following week, with no apologies for the delay. He had separately ordered steel ball-bearings to load the gun with and researched online on ways to improve the power of the weapon. It would be illegal, but his plans did not involve humans, so in his mind; totally justified.

Over the next two days, he tested his modifications. It impressed him that the gun could now shoot right through both sides of aluminium cans and completely shattering his old vinyl records. His living room was a mess of broken plastic and discarded ball-bearings. It was worth it. He was ready. He smiled at his own genius.

The next day he tucked the gun into the rear of his jeans, gangsta-style. He grinned as he biked through Cleethorpes, determined to eliminate the birds that terrified him daily. George made his way on to the wall, taking in the low tide as it made it look possible to walk across the Humber to the neighbouring city, Hull. Such a view had no right being spoiled by the ornithological twats.

He glared from a distance as he saw them circling and swooping outside the factory. He sped up, pulling the gun from his waistband and holding it steadily in front, he squinted, aiming and following the lowest bird he saw. Then he fired.

The recoil was stronger than he'd anticipated, pushing his arm backwards and turning his shoulders, jerking the handlebars, forcing the bike into a collusion with the wall. It propelled George over the handlebars, face first into the concrete. The collision twixt face and floor separated the vertebrae in his neck, leaving him paralysed, but twitching on the bird-shit stained path. Consciousness faded as he watched a gull land and cocked its head quizzically at him. His last thought was, 'stay away from my eyes, dickhead'. His wishes would not come true.

Donkey

Broken down. Knackered. Flea-bitten. Adjectives all used to describe Albert's donkey on Cleethorpes beach. It seemed to many that he'd been stood there with Gracie, the donkey, for almost a hundred years. They were way off. By almost two millennia.

Albert recalled being stood there the day the Vikings landed on the shores of the Humber Estuary, his name then something he was unable to recall. Albert, as the locals called him, had a mind that frequently failed him as much as Gracie emptied her bowels. Thousands of years-worth of events tended to get muddled together in the mind; often pushed out completely.

There'd been women in his life. Many, many women. The one that stood the test of time, enduring despite his failing thoughts, was the memory of one woman from the Viking days. Her name was Frigg, a flaxen-haired beauty, cheeks redeemed by the cold air from the frigid trip across the North Sea. It'd been love at first sight.

Or lust, either way he'd been keen to get to know her.

She'd spent several years in his company, content, but occasionally complaining in Germanic grunts about the attention he paid to Gracie. Other than that minor quibble, they'd been ecstatic together. Until one fateful day.

Albert (or whatever his name back then) was posted at his usual spot, by the pier (which had yet to be built). Another boat came in, this time containing a woman, larger in stature than Frigg, but with flame-red hair, an unusual sight in those days. Their eyes locked, and within moments, so were their limbs in an aggressive coupling in the sand.

As he threw his head back; the vinegar strokes pumping his load into her, Albert's eyes opened and he saw Frigg, standing where the cockle store now resides. Fury and tears in her eyes, she spat on Albert as she stomped passed him and into the departing ship, never to be seen again.

Albert's wistful musings turned the day into night. It began to rain, so he took shelter under the pier, thinking about his precious Frigg and desperately wanting the chance for her to appear, for him to apologise. Albert gazed at Gracie, he drew his shoulders into his chest as the wind picked up. Gracie's ears twitched in annoyance as clouds of sand coated them both. Albert winced and rubbed the flecks from his eyes.

As he blinked, he rubbed his eyes once again. She'd returned. His beloved Frigg, smiling, eyes soft, hinting at forgiveness. He stammered out his apologies, but she silenced him with a deft touch from her fingers to his lips. She drew him into her embrace, inching her face closer to his. She was still as beautiful to Albert as the day she left in anger. He, in contrast, was an unravelled, wizened shell of his former self. His self-consciousness faded as Frigg kissed him. The kiss was a long, lingering and powerful probing. It stirred his loins in a way that had not happened in an age.

Frigg removed her dress, revealing unblemished skin, exuding a heat that warmed Albert, despite the cold rain cocooning his makeshift shelter under the pier. She tugged at his waistband, urgency in her eyes. Albert freed his tumescence, and she guided him inside her, an action that elicited a soft moan from her, increasing Albert's ardour.

Wrapped in each other, Albert thrusted with the enthusiasm of a teen. Frigg's eyes appeared to demand more; more power, more intensity. From within, Albert summoned more strength into his ministrations, trying with increasing passion to satisfy her. Still, she demanded more. His thrust became more violent, shifting both of their bodies further up the beach. His gyrations became violent, seemingly a hatefuck, until they became an unnatural blur. Frigg's gasps and almost mocking smile became too much for the old man and he pumped his first load in over two hundred years, eyes rolling back in his head as he did so.

Recovering from his coital ecstasy, covered in sweat and send, he was alarmed to see Frigg stood at his side, fully clothed once again, a cruel sneer dancing across her face. He looked down, the slickness on his belly he'd wrongly assumed to be sweat, revealed to be blood. He groaned, knowing when Frigg motioned to his left what he would see. Gracie, twitching, bleeding on the sand. He'd fucked his donkey to death. Frigg had taken her revenge.

Her vengeance was not complete, however. With a wave of her hand, Gracie's corpse revealed its true form—the red-headed

21

woman. Albert memories returned with a jolt, as if someone had lifted a veil. Her name was Grayseed. Frigg smirked as the realisation dawned on him, yet appeared pensive, studying his actions as if expecting something. Albert's final realisation. His name wasn't Albert... it was Odin.

Odin regained his faculties and felt his power slowly return. Frigg snapped her fingers and Odin dropped to the beach, unconscious. She knelt by him and touched his head. He wouldn't remember this. Then she paced purposefully towards Grayseed's body.

Albert awoke, confused underneath Cleethorpes pier. He'd fallen asleep on the beach again. It comes with age; he supposed. He trudged his way towards the Ferris wheel. Another day of work. Gracie trotted to his side.

-    At least I've still got you, girl.

Untitled Document.

He placed his laptop on the new desk in the spare bedroom. He'd recently purchased a terraced property with an inheritance from a deceased relative. He'd quit his job because of the sizable nature of the windfall and pursued a career as a writer. He was in his mid-twenties, so changing career was not as much of a gamble as it would be later in life. He'd despised his previous job, so the inheritance proved merely a catalyst that prompted a decision that crossed his mind for every minute of his eight-hour days.

'No distractions', he told himself as he booted up his laptop with excitement, eager to begin what he envisioned would be a new chapter in his life, one that would earn respect and recognition. He'd no idea what to write about, but according to advice he'd read online he should 'just sit down and write'. The word processing programme flickered into life and a fresh, blank document glowed in front of him, beckoning the words from his mind. He placed his fingers lightly on the keypad and waited for the words to come.

Something was wrong. He appeared to have forgotten all the words in the English language and seemed unable to summon them forth to kick-start his latest endeavour. He withdrew his hands to his side and pondered on why he was unable to think of a beginning. He concluded that tension caused his blockage. He needed music, the perfect way to relax himself and open the floodgates that would no doubt one day lead to multiple awards. He ran downstairs to grab his Bluetooth speaker and hurriedly plugged it in, resting it on a nearby shelf. He connected his phone to the speaker and began to play a random selection of tunes from the list of over a thousand saved onto his phone. He grinned as he sat back down enjoying the ambience and poised himself over the laptop once again.

Still the words wouldn't come, the blank page began to seem as if it were mocking him, a white slab of failure before he'd even begun. He needed inspiration but didn't know where to find it. He decided to read some articles online to gain some sort of idea on what to base his writing on. He didn't recall having this problem writing stories as a child. He started with the daily news, scrolling through headlines looking for a subject, not even as the basis of the story, but something that might work via metaphor.

Two hours later, he put his phone down, frustrated. He still had nothing. He'd managed to fit in a heated debate on immigration with some illiterate right-wingers in a comments thread, discovered a possibility of various cancers based on an emerging spot on his arm and was up to date with all the latest memes. The words 'untitled document' glared at him accusingly and he opted to go for a rare cigarette outside and make himself a cup of tea. Perhaps the fresh air would help. He stood in the small porch, prolonging the cigarette and smoking it right down to the filter, he fought with his mind in desperation for any subject. He knew it was there, but it just wouldn't come. The warming May rains cocooned his property, promising a hot summer soon. Despite this, he shuddered as if cold and decided not to smoke the second cigarette as planned. He returned indoors and made a tea in the over-sized mug he saved for when he didn't want to be running back and forth to the kitchen.

As he returned to his makeshift study, music still blaring, it startled him to discover words appearing on his laptop's screen. A constant barrage causing the page to constantly scroll down, try as he might, it was impossible to read and concentrate on the words being written whilst it moved. He stepped back, curious as to what was going on. He touched the mouse and clicked 'save'. The words stopped, and he clicked 'OK' to save as an untitled document. He scanned the screen for any clue why this had happened and the writing began again. With a sigh, he assumed what was going on. One of his friends must have accessed his laptop remotely and was playing a prank on him. As the screen began to fill up once more, he left the room and trudged back downstairs to switch off the Wi-Fi, disconnecting them from his computer.

Jogging back upstairs, expecting that the denied internet to have ended the access to his PC; puzzled to notice it hadn't. The screen filled just as rapidly as before, word count in the two-thousands and rising. He reached over to his mouse and in doing so, noticed the screen freezing midway through a word. The icon to centralise briefly flashed, followed by the bold icon and finishing up on the resize text menu, stopping on twenty.

Leave it alone. Let me work.

He jumped back from the screen alarmed onto his chair, which moved back from the force, colliding his head with the shelf, causing the Bluetooth speaker to fall, also landing on his head with a dull 'thunk'. He replaced the speaker, still blasting tunes at high volume as if oblivious to what was happening. His hand began rubbing the sore parts of his head, he stared at the screen. The words ordering him to leave it alone deleted themselves and the story continued. He stood up and checked his phone to see if the Bluetooth on the laptop was turned on, the last possible way another person remained connected to it. His mouth clucked with impatience as he waited for his phone to connect, only to be met with the message; 'device is not currently activated'.

He stared at the screen in disbelief. Unable to think of another way a person could be able to control his computer with no internet access and no Bluetooth. With the word count creeping towards three thousand words; this must be an elaborate prank. He began to feel afraid, because of the lack of a logical explanation for what unfolded before him. To no one in particular, he posed the only question that sprang to mind.

-   What in the fuck is going on?

His words, lost in the music playing at volume beside him, forced him to question if he'd spoken them aloud. He stared at the screen, filling with words still and slumped down in the chair, fear turning to confusion as he toyed with ideas.

27

His mind still as blank as the pages previously were on his computer. He remained sat, motionless, staring intently at his laptop screen, watching the word count steadily increase.

'Perhaps this is some kind of dormant psychokinetic ability?' he thought to himself. Formerly, he would have dismissed something like this as pure fiction, or just plain mental. Now, with the remarkable happening before his eyes, he'd no choice but to consider such a notion. He'd ruled out outside access, what else could it be? What added to his theory of the bizarre situation being an 'ability' was that he'd sat willing himself to write only a short time ago. He imagined that, somehow, he drew the words from within himself and made them appear on the screen.

The story continued at a pace in front of him, calming him as he considered himself in no danger. As he watched, he had visions of literary recognition for works he'd never typed, or indeed consciously thought of. He fantasised about fame, perhaps TV or film adaptations of his work. He mused carefully over what to say on the talk shows, how humble he would appear and the sage advice he'd offer to other aspiring writers. His excitement mounted about the possibilities.

Excited to read his work for the first time when finished.

Hours passed by and the word count approached eight thousand. The room grew dark, and he experienced pangs of hunger accompanied by boredom. He reached for the phone to stop the looped music, something that would go forever providing it still had power. He stopped himself, worried that by changing anything about the current set up, it would break the cycle and prevent the writing continuing. He grabbed his phone charger from the other room with haste, afraid that it needed his presence for it all to carry on. He was relieved to note that it wasn't as it continued in his absence. His trembling hands forced the phone charger into the plug socket, connecting the lead to his phone. He backed away slowly, ensuring that nothing changed. Satisfied, he made his way downstairs to the kitchen and prepared himself a meal.

His mind raced. He couldn't focus on his food, only the strange situation he found himself in and what to do afterwards. His excitement was like a child on a hundred Christmas Eves at once. He tried to watch TV, but his mind strayed too often from on-screen events. It began to concern him; it proved too difficult sit and watch the words appear as he couldn't read it as it was being written. He set up his games console and tried to distract himself that way. It worked for a time until his eyelids grew heavy and he retired to bed for the night.

Sleep proved impossible due to a combination of loud music and his own mind's inability to 'switch off'. A neighbour banged on the walls, the universal gesture for 'turn that fucking music off now!' He refused to do it. To mitigate the disturbance, he gathered up a few foam pieces that'd been left in the property and taped them to the wall surrounding the speakers and then fixed several pieces to the door. He closed the door with trepidation, then opened it again quickly to check that everything remained as it should be. Relieved that nothing had stopped, he closed the door and attempted once again to sleep.

Still sleep would not come, the foam pieces had muffled the noise, but not enough so he couldn't hear it entirely. He strained to hear which songs played through the dulled sound and his ability to sleep further marred by the game of his own creation. He wrapped the duvet tightly around his head in a vain attempt to block out any distractions. This was fruitless, so desperately, he resorted to the well-stocked drinks cabinet he kept in case of emergency social event.

He poured a small glass of brandy and quickly knocked it back. It would be a waste of time to keep pouring it, so he took the bottle back up to his room with him and silently took slugs from it, whilst trying, unsuccessfully, to concentrate on the television. His plan eventually worked, he passed out into a drunken slumber for a moment. A crash that shook the house and pounded his skull woke him. Groggily, he ran towards the makeshift office to check everything was OK, banging his feet on furniture as he stumbled, co-ordination dulled by the consumption of a half-bottle of brandy. Curses trailed from his lips as he burst into the office, his anxiety dissipated by the sight of words still being manifested by whatever force. He struggled intently to focus on the word count. Eighteen thousand.

- How long is this going to be?

He grumbled out loud as he checked the house, draped in a duvet for the source of the noise that woke him. He couldn't find a thing out of place. With a shrug, he staggered back to bed putting it down to imagination. He grabbed the heavily dented bottle of brandy and took another swig. He was tired and longed for sleep.

Thus, began his life over the next three days. He drank heavily to prompt sleep, then woken by a noise. Sometimes a bang or thud, sometimes a screech. Over this time, sobriety and he were no longer friend. He'd check the laptop, the rest of the house, then drink again to try to gain some sleep. Over these three days, he barely had a total of an hour's sleep, he feared hallucinations and prayed for it to be over soon.

Finally, mercifully, it stopped. Again, he disturbed by a huge thud, this time, the source clear to him. The door to the office had been flung open, as he creeped towards the computer, he saw no movement. The screen simply read, 'Chapter 1'; the beginning of the document. The word count showed over eighty thousand words. It was complete! The disturbing fact that the door slammed open of its own accord, discarded from his mind by the adrenaline of finally seeing what the ordeal produced. He saved the document, still untitled since he'd no idea what it said yet. He stopped the music, his favourite tunes had started to grate on him considerably. The ensuing silence pierced his ears, and he mildly recoiled from the change in aural environment. With a shake of his head to clear it, he pulled up the chair and began to read.

The toll of the previous days soon caught up with him. The lack of sleep, combined with his drunken state meant that despite his best efforts, squinting and closing one eye at a time, he was unable to stay awake to read the document. His head hung low into his chest as he drifted into a dreamless slumber. There he sat for the next seven hours until awoken by screaming.

He panicked and jolted out of the chair. As he covered his mouth, he realised that the screaming that had woken him came from his own lips. He glared accusingly at the empty bottle nearby. Shaken, he staggered downstairs to brew himself a coffee and take a handful of painkillers for the monstrous hangover he now suffered from. He caught a whiff of himself and elected to shower for the first time in four days. Refreshed, he sat back in the chair to finally read what had caused his malaise.

Despite his throbbing head, he was rapidly immersed in the prose. In his mind, it was nothing short of brilliant. It featured two protagonists, one a detective investigating the murder of the other. Each chapter flit deftly between one story and the other, mirroring the events of each one as the victim's life unfolded and suspects were introduced. The detective was dogged, with an ego that refused to be beaten, despite the insurmountable odds. As one character's life began to spiral out of control, the detective became closer to uncover what had happened. Then, abruptly, the words ceased.

He shouted in frustration. Whilst reading the novel, he'd almost forgotten what led him to this point, lost as he'd been in the sheer entertainment the book had provided. He thought the book was the best thing he'd ever read and was eager for the end. He let out a sob of frustration as he banged his hand down on the desk which prompted text to appear on the screen.

Finish it.

He stared at the text for a moment until it eventually disappeared. He understood. Scrolling back to the beginning of the document, he began reading again to see where he considered it would end. He figured that three chapters remained to complete the tale, one where the detective figured out and revealed the identity of the killer, one where the victim met his end, and the denouement and aftermath. Was this a test? He was unsure as he started to work on his own version of the ending.

For hours he sat, rapidly typing, occasionally pausing to consult notes he had scribbled about each character. He carefully ensured to make no errors as he worked; it would be an insult to the rest of the book if he elected to edit them later. After seven hours of beavering on the chapters, they were complete. He beamed with pride as he clicked save. He looked at the title—still Untitled Document. He resolved to spend the next few days coming up with a name worthy of such a masterpiece. Startled by a crashing sound coming from the walls surrounding him, he jolted out of the chair, head jerking violently with panic. The noise was relentless as if a thousand hammers assaulted the walls from within. Eyes wide with terror, he covered his ears with his hands and stood, unsure of what to do. Then, as suddenly as it began, the crashing stopped. He breathlessly steadied himself, trying to regain composure. His eyes chanced upon the screen.

- No! No! No! Nononononononooooo!

His work had disappeared, the rest of the document remained, minus the final chapters. Text appeared back onto the screen.

Finish it.

He howled with frustration and punched the wall, causing much pain to himself, but nary a mark on the wall. His thoughts went back to this being a cruel prank. Somehow, someone watched him. He darted around the house, closing every blind and curtain, ensuring that the Wi-Fi router remained switched off, and finally placing a piece of masking tape over the camera on the laptop. The text again faded from view. Maybe he had been looking at this wrong? Perhaps it wasn't a prank, could this be a spirit telling its tale, asking him to solve the murder? A hacky ending for such an intricate work, but he had to rule out the possibility. He reluctantly turned the router back on and began to search for character names and murders. He came up with nothing.

His frazzled mind returned to the theory that this was some sort of cosmic writing test that he'd failed. He complied with the on-screen prompts and try a different ending. Rushing through this time, he finished in four hours, less satisfied with the result, but closer to where he thought the clues may lay. Again, the same circumstances played out; noise, followed by his fear and his words ceasing to exist.

Finish it.

His hands ached from typing and the injury he'd done to the wall. He was out of painkillers and needed a stiff drink. He threw on a coat and headed to the shop to resupply himself with both. He came back loaded down with four carrier bags, all of which contained alcohol and cigarettes. The brand names on the bottles were gone, replaced simply by the name of the product in the largest letters on each bottle. Whiskey, Brandy, Rum; he had gone for quantity over quality. He swore loudly as he unpacked the shopping. He'd forgotten the painkillers. He wasn't going back. He took one full bag up to his makeshift study and prepared to battle once again with the missing end.

As he took healthy swigs from whichever bottle stood closest to his reach, he noticed the pain was almost gone. He tapped away, no longer even giving a cursory look to check spelling or grammar, he simply wanted to finish. He paused for a second as he thought he smelled shit. He shoved his hand down the back of his jeans and pulled it out quickly. He stared at his fingers, no trace, he hadn't shit himself. He scanned the room and saw nothing that indicated the foul odour. He shrugged and elected to simply breathe through his mouth.

Finish it.

This attempt was the same as the first two. The noise, followed by a milder panic than before, since he expected it, then the deletion of his text. Grim determination took over him. He wouldn't leave this room until it was finished. He read the entire story again, looking for patterns in the detective's story that may point at following or previous chapters for nods in the right direction. It was so intricately written that he assumed this was the case. Yet as he examined it more closely, each supposed revelation he found, would contradict something explicitly stated elsewhere. He tried again with a new ending based on some new clues he'd gathered, regardless of if it fit. Was this intricate or contrived?

Finish it.

The shit aroma got worse. He tried a Stephen King ending; an ex-machina solution.

Finish it.

The weeks carried on; he tried every conceivable ending he'd the ability to think of. Aliens invaded; the world blew up. The detective was the victim's father. The detective did it. The butler that'd never been featured did it. The reek of shit grew worse, he couldn't find a source. He drank through his entire supply of alcohol over these weeks and simply quit smoking when the cigarettes ran out, the empty bottles used as makeshift ashtrays. Every time he fell asleep, he awoke screaming at night terrors he could never remember. Every time he completed a draft, the same thing happened without fail.

Finish it.

Finish it.

Finish it.

Finish it.

He slumped at the desk, beaten. He had no ideas left, nor any energy to lift his head. He just wanted to sleep.

-   I can't do it.

He said the words out loud and then began to giggle manically. He'd located the source of the feculent aroma. It was his own breath. He closed his eyes and then fell still.

It was further weeks before the house shook with thumps as police used a ram on the door. He hadn't been seen on over two months and the neighbours had reported the smell. The wood around the door frame splintered as the police made their way in, shouting requests for his well-being that wouldn't be answered. They found his corpse slumped over the desk, surrounded by empty bottles and scribbled notes, clothes hanging to his malnourished and decomposing frame.

The laptop remained switched on, still titled Untitled Document. The word count read six.

Leave me alone. Let me work.

No Clip

Winner of the Globe writer's Halloween short story competition.

Grifffromdamarsh: So how the fuck does that make me an SJW cuck?

Def2noobs: Keep crying PC baby

Weeb4lyf: rollingeyes.emoji

Grifffromdamarsh: Spawn camping is what losers do, all I'm saying.

Def2noobs: 1v1 me then, fag.

Grifffromdamarsh: Sure. No spawn camping or GTFO

Weeb4lyf: donkeyface.emoji donkeyface.emoji pepethefroggrin.emoji

Brian sighed. He'd been plugging away on Twitch for two months now, trying to establish himself on the platform. Broadcasting himself playing video games seemed like a dream to him. His audience was slowly growing, but not at the rate he'd like. Not at the rate needed for the illustrious Twitch partnership programme; the next step in making his hobby a potential career. Brian watched the chat monitor scrolling through as Griff and Def bickered. They were his most regular viewers, and also his most toxic. They berated him daily, criticising his abilities, posting insults (disguised as 'banter') and, worst of all, back-seating. Once he'd his own mods, those two in particular were heading for the ban-hammer.

A garish pink neon outlined a cartoon cat on the screen. The cat wore shades, the shorthand for cool, and pointed at a glowing purple sign behind it; 'Kat-Chan will be airing soon!'. The cartoon cat also sported a duster coat. Brian looked at the image, his placeholder before starting his streams, and wondered if he should ask the artist to add a fedora.

Grifffromdamarsh: Where the fuck is Kat, anyway? Fucking amateur streamers man. So unprofessional.

Def2noobs: Yeah, you're a busy guy. You've got Cheetos to eat, Mountain Dew to drink and masturbatin' to do. YeeHaw. 'Murrca

Grifffromdamarsh: At least I have all my teeth, Brit fag.

Weeb4lyf: isaaccrying.emoji stfu.emoji.

Brian screwed his eyes and drew in a breath. On his main monitor, he readied the game and the software he would use for tonight's stream. He would try something a little different; to explore the out-of-bounds content of a horror game he'd previously played; Mirabelle. Mirabelle was an atmospheric first-person puzzler set in a mansion controlled by a demonic porcelain doll. As ideas went, it was certainly derivative, but something about the game had chilled Brian to his core, much to the delight of his viewers, relishing in his every squirm, erupting into laughter and a sea of emojis at his screams at the jump-scares. It was also, to date, his highest viewed stream, with edited highlights performing well on YouTube as well.

Steeling himself, Brian clicked on the icon to start his stream. His image appeared in the bottom-left corner of the screen. Brian smiled as warm and welcoming as he could fake towards the regulars already in the chat.

- Hey guys! Thanks for waiting! Got something special in mind for tonight's stream!

Def2noobs: About fucking time.

Grifffromdamarsh: I should punish you for your re-tardiness.

Weeb4lyf: prayinghands.emoji

Brian booted up the Mirabelle game from his launcher. He tried to engage with the chat as best he could without losing his temper at the entitled pricks he depended on to kick-start the rest of his audience engagement. An active chat, no matter how hostile, was encouraging to other interested parties. Streaming was not just about the content, but also the community. The view count number rose from three to seven as the Mirabelle logo filled the screen, accompanied by the sounds of thunder and icy screams.

Grifffromdamarsh: No, fuck that dude. You've already done this game. This is just lazy. It doesn't change. Play something else.

Def2noobs: For once, I agree with the dickhead. Fuck walking simulators. They are boring as shit.

Weeb4lyf: kappa.emoji kappa.emoji ?

- No Weeb, I'm not trolling. Relax guys. It isn't a straight play through, I've got some no-clip software, and I was going to run a boundary break of the game.

Def2noobs: I'll allow it. For now.

Grifffromdamarsh: OK. At least we get to laugh at your girlie squeals.

Weeb4lyf: shrug.emoji

Brian resisted the urge to glower. If these guys hated him so much, why did they show up every night? He wished they would give him something, anything, that indicated they liked him in some way. Weeb seemed OK, but only ever communicated in emojis, almost a new language he'd had to adapt to. Brian clicked the 'start game' button on screen, the motionless titular dolls porcelain lips twisting into a malevolent grin and the screen zooms into the eye, fizzling into white noise and the opening cinematic began. Whilst this played, Brian activated the no clip software, minimizing the box and placing it on the lower-right corner of the screen. The viewer count grew from seven to twelve. Strangely, only the three regulars were active in the chat.

Weeb4lyf: spookyskeleton.emoji

Grifffromdamarsh: How2hack for boomers :D

Def2noobs: Where's the dubstep? Bwwwwwaaaaaaarrrrrggghhh

Brian ignored the jibes and progressed through the introduction of the game, waiting for the entry to the mansion for the boundary breaking software fun to begin. The first-person perspective on the screen flickered as the character's arms strained to push open the heavy wooden doors with an ominous creak. The camera perspective changed to a second-person viewpoint as eyes watched the protagonist walk with trepidation into the huge, open hallway. As the camera shifted once more, it becomes clear, through the aid of lightning effects that the second viewpoint was that of the titular doll; motionless in a glass display cabinet. Windows glowing with moonlight reflected on the china cheeks of Mirabelle. The doll's clothes were ragged and aged, a mixture of whites, sepia browns and fag-ash yellow. Patches of hair were missing from the doll's scalp, perhaps lost to the passage of time. The character leans in for a closer inspection when a lightning flashes, creating the illusion that the lifeless eyes flick directly to the player. Despite himself, Brian flinched at the jump-scare, cursing as he did so.

- Fucks sake! I knew it was coming too!

Grifffromdamarsh: Hahahahahahahahahha!

Def2noobs: Gotta admit, as boring as this game is, it nailed those lighting effects.

Weeb4lyf: pants.emoji poop.emoji

- Ok guys! Let's take a look through the walls, see what's there!

Brian's enforced comradery caused derision from his regular viewers. The view count grew further, now showing thirty-five watching. On screen, the first-person perspective headed straight towards a wall adorned with a faded green wallpaper with cracked and peeling Fleur-de-Lys symbols in a diagonal pattern. The symbols filled the screen, betraying their jpeg origins, before it filled the screen with black, the reverse images of walls and doors to the character's right-hand side. Brian moved the character forwards, towards the location of the first of the game's scares, one that sees the titular doll running across the player's pathway accompanied by the giggle of a child.

Since the character was out of bounds, the audio cues had no point of reference, so once the background music reached the end, it could no longer loop. The silence echoed as Brian pitched forward into darkness, a small room emerging from the gloom and slowly filling the screen.

Grifffromdamarsh: This is dull. I'm starting a petition to change the game.

Weeb4lyf: hush.emoji

A wood panelled wall filled the screen, before Brian pushed through into the room. He flicked the camera around to check the surroundings; nothing out of the ordinary. He focussed the camera on the image of Mirabelle, the character model in the standard pose; upright with arms stretched outwards to the side, a bastardised version of a crucifixion. Brian opened his mouth to speak with his viewers, but a glitch caused the child's laughter to cue, causing a yelp of fright.

- So gu—yaaarrgggh!

Weeb4lyf: lmfao.emoji

Def2noobs: Oooohhh! The jump-scares are in slightly different places. Change the game please.

Grifffromdamarsh: I don't think Kat will, the view count has just reached 104. Your best stream ever?

- I... I... hadn't noticed. But, yeah Griff, you're right. Hey to all the new viewers!

Brian scolded himself for being so jumpy. But it made for entertaining viewing at least. He used the controller to zoom in to the doll, trying to pan around to get a close-up of the face.

Frustratingly, the camera wouldn't obey his commands, hitting an invisible wall as the sides of the head became visible. This confused Brian, there should be no walls at all with no clip software. He tried to back out of the room to enter from another angle. Strange. The character appeared to be now trapped inside the small room. Brian placed his controller down as his hands operated the mouse and keyboard, re-running the software and searching for a reason it had stopped working online.

Grifffromdamarsh: Yaaaaawwwwwwwwnnnn!

Def2noobs: Again, we agree. This guy ain't getting his hacking badge from the scouts.

Weeb4lyf: look.emoji

With Brian distracted and frustrated, skim reading search results for a solution, the outstretched arms of Mirabelle moved. At first, almost infinitesimally, but picking up speed to a crawl. The arms lowered as the doll glided forward, the blank expression becoming a grimace as a flat, deep voice filled Brian's headphones.

You're not supposed to be in here.

Brian didn't scream, beads of cold perspiration formed on his head. His eyes widened, glassing with tears of terror. The voice vibrated though his skull and felt as if he'd swallowed the words, causing his guts to churn. He wanted to wrench the headphones from himself and throw them against the wall and exit the game, but it froze him to his seat, seemingly mesmerised by what unfurled on the screen before him. The doll's mouth twisted into a grin. This elicited a physical response from Brian as he jumped, jerking his gaming chair to the left by two feet. The doll's eyes on screen followed his movement. Curiosity, though, tinged with fear, caused him to move side to side. Still the doll's eyes matched his movement. Brian shivered. Sod the stream, he was turning it off. He noticed the view count; 234. His best stream ever and he was disconnecting. His hand crept towards the escape key. The doll's brow furrowed.

Mirabelle1: I wouldn't do that if I were you.

Mirabelle2: I wouldn't do that if I were you.

Mirabelle3: I wouldn't do that if I were you.

Mirabelle4: I wouldn't do that if I were you.

Grifffromdamarsh: What the fuck is going on?

Mirabelle5: I wouldn't do that if I were you.

Mirabelle6: I wouldn't do that if I were you.

Weeb4lyf: shrug.emoji spooked.emoji

Mirabelle7: I wouldn't do that if I were you.

Mirabelle8: I wouldn't do that if I were you.

Def2noobs: This is a cool effect Kat, how did you do it?

The chat screen flared into life, dominated by variants of the Mirabelle bot flooding his screen with his regulars, questioning what he'd done. He closed his eyes, finger hovering over the escape key, his breathing jagged and shallow. Why was he so scared? What was the worst that could happen? The chat screen continued.

Mirabelle232: I wouldn't do that if I were you.

Mirabelle233: I wouldn't do that if I were you.

Brian gritted his teeth and stabbed the escape key. The image on the screen began to fizzle and pop.

Mirabelle234: I warned you.

Static filled the screen, flickering between the black and white fuzz and the leering face of the video game doll. A piercing squeak of what sounded like a rusty swing filled the headphones of Brian and his viewers alike. A disorienting flickering grew rapid, becoming a strobe like effect. The webcam image of Brian, mouth widening in horror, tears spilling from his eyes, cowering in a strobe-induced twelve frames per second. The screen went blank suddenly, as the programme closed-down, Brian's image disappeared from view, replaced by only darkness.

Grifffromdamarsh: OK. I admit. That was pretty cool.

Def2noobs: And original. Well done Kat!

Weeb4lyf: applause.emoji

Brian's wallpaper backdrop appeared on screen, a white background with anime waifus in a variety of suggestive poses. The glow from the screen illuminated his image in the screen's corner. His head was bowed, a trickle of drool hanging from his mouth. Brian started to cackle, his head raising slowly as he stared into the camera. His eyes widened and his mouth widened into a wet, menacing smile. He inched towards the camera.

- Stay tuned folks! You're next!

Brian pulled his hand back and swiped at the camera, disconnecting his image from the feed. The placeholder returned. The viewer counter showed 3.

Grifffromdamarsh: Short, but definitely sweet.

Def2noobs: Yeah, it's great when streamers get creative. I'm sharing this as we speak.

Weeb4lyf: Yes, we should all do that. Share it now.

Lions Loose in Grimsby!

i.

With the Levellers playing at high volume on his Walkman, Charlie strode down the road leading to where Hewitt's circus had set up for a few days. He wasn't going to watch the clowns, nor the acrobats. He certainly didn't want to meet the lion tamer, but he had an interest in the lions. Despite him and his group's ineffectual protests, the show would go ahead as planned for another year. He despised the way circuses used and abused animals for entertainment. It seemed cruel and needed stopping. It had no place in the 90s.

He'd recently left college and disappointed his family by not continuing onto university. He didn't want to be a part of 'the system' that rolled out more and more capitalist pigs as time passed by. Charlie perceived himself as breaking the cycle, forging ahead to a new world, regressive and progressive at the same time. Why use money to pay for goods, when it's possible to grow goods and trade them? His logic always fell apart when he tried to pay for a pack of Embassy with a pound of carrots.

He had met up with like-minded people at college. By like-minded, that is to say, they seemed confident and assured of their beliefs, so he sailed along for the ride. Initially, they mocked him for his middle-class name. He didn't have a defence, because, quite simply put, he was definitely middle-class. Raised in Humberston, he'd wanted for nothing growing up, his family even saving a considerable amount to help him through university. He'd demanded they release that money to him since he'd no intention of going, but they insisted on holding on to it 'just in case he changed his mind'. Charlie loved his family, but viewed them as blind sheep, following the rules without question. He would try to wake them up over time.

His group of ragtag individuals warmed to him a great deal after his first hunt sabotage. The act of disrupting the pursuit of foxes was one thing that he looked forward to. They distracted the beagles with food and would spend an entire day being a general nuisance to the pursuers. Sky, one of the more headstrong women in the group, had broken away and lashed a gate together with hemp rope when one hunter dismounted and approached her with menace, riding crop in hand. To her credit, she didn't flinch and screamed a torrent of abuse at her potential attacker. Charlie had spotted this and sprinted over to her aid. He tackled the hunter, clad in a red hunting jacket, and began wailing on him from the mounted position. Or to put it the way it would be described later, he 'battered the toff'. The mischievous grin and twinkle in Sky's eyes after he had done this melted his heart, Charlie though that it was that moment, splattered with the blood from the burst nose of a rich prick, in which he fell in love with her.

His place in the group cemented, he started wearing nothing but combat shorts, mud-caked timberlands and a patchwork hoodie he'd found on sale in C&A. He watched news reports of similarly dressed protesters camping in tress across the UK to prevent motorways or buildings. Charlie foretold of an uprising and remained keen to be a part of it. He shaved his head all but a small circle of hair on the crown of his skull, which he'd grown into a single dreadlock. Sky, drunk one night had remarked that she thought his change looked awesome, then kissed him tenderly, before having to leave. He wanted more of that, he wanted her to be his girlfriend and dreamed of having sex with her. Maybe after a bath, he wasn't sure.

It was that desire to impress that led him to today's solo mission. He wanted to free the enslaved creatures and deal a blow to the circus at the same time. Perhaps if this happened each year, they would at least take the animal portion out of their shows because of the hassle. He wouldn't find circuses that bothersome then, other than they were complete shit. With his imagination teasing images of Sky's eyes lighting up on hearing the news dancing through his head, he clambered over the perimeter fence. The circus staff bustled, all focussed on preparations for the evening's show, applying make up to the clowns and testing ropes and harnesses for weakness. 'Fucking carnies.' Charlie thought, 'why don't they get a proper job?' With stealth, he rounded the back of the caravans to where he ascertained from the smell, that the animals were kept. All he spotted were four lions, depressing him to his core. In two cages, barely able to contain their bulk, stood two lions in each. The lions uncomfortably shifted against each other and the bars, trying to at least lay down in comfort. He looked in their eyes and they didn't respond. Charlie considered he'd never seen true sadness on anything in his short life until that moment. It sickened him to his core and steeled his resolve.

He removed bolt cutters from his yellow Army Surplus bag, scrawled with anarchic slogans to express his individuality, like the rest of his friends. With no small amount of effort, he cut through the padlocks on the front of the cages and flung them open wide. Three of the lions bolted out of the cages, sprinting towards the centre of the caravan's semi-circle. Charlie heard shouts of alarm from behind him, but focussed on the remaining lion, paws in front of it, heavily maned head resting forlornly on top of them. "Come on guy, you're free, you don't have to be here anymore" he crooned in a soft voice as he stood next to the cage. He reached through the bars and patted the lion's side in a gentle manner and gestured towards the sound of the screams.

Charlie opened the door wider and whilst doing so, moved forwards to peer through the cracks in the mobile dwellings to determine how long he had to make his escape. He spotted a clown, lying still on the floor staring at him accusingly with glassy eyes. Panic began to take a hold of his mind as the gravity of what he'd done sank in. This was short lived as the second thing to sink into him was the fangs of the beast behind him as it pounced on his back, clamping its huge jaws onto his collarbone and shaking him like a rag doll. He yelled in pain as it tossed him around the area, claws tearing through his woollen top and severing arteries in his legs. After what seemed like an eternity, the lion stopped, sniffing at his twitching body and padded off toward the others.

Charlie had been conscious through the entire ordeal, but strangely, he no longer felt any pain. He observed the grass painted red with his blood and knew that it wasn't a good sign. Three deep gashes caused by claw swipes had decimated his face and torn out his right eye. With his left eye he gazed at the empty cages and once again imagined Sky's eyes, this time filling with tears as she learned about his sacrifice. It would make her determination increase, he knew that. As his left eye closed for the final time, he told himself, 'I didn't really think this through'.

ii.

Fifteen-year-old Billy sat on the windowsill of his bedroom, large window ajar, smoking a cigarette stolen from his mother's packet downstairs. As he looked at the identical housing of the Willows estate, formerly all council owned properties, he considered himself king of the area.

His pals would often congregate around the corner from his house on two brickwork mounds, originally built for the skateboarding craze of the early 80s. The mounds proved useless for skating as the children found in their earlier years, as the uneven bricks, separated with loose mortar would catch on the wheels and send them flying, chin first to the grey concrete paving slabs. Their only real use was for sitting on and smoking.

Billy spied a police officer walking down the pathway past his house. He flicked the finished cigarette and leaned outside, swinging his right hand in a wanker gesture and screamed, "BELLEND!" He had done this for the benefit of his friend and neighbour Mike, who noticed him and began to giggle hysterically. The police officer turned around glaring at Billy, then walked towards his front door. Billy's eyes widened, and he dove onto his bed panicking. The officer was a woman, Billy considered her quite a pretty one too, despite her short hair. He began to imagine how she would punish him; his hand began to stray down his pants for the third time that morning when a knock on the door jolted him back into the moment.

Billy's mother had heard him scream and had started up the stairs to admonish him when, she too, was interrupted by the knock on the door. With a curse, she turned her considerable bulk and made her way back down to answer the door. Upon seeing the officer, she rolled her eyes and invited her inside. She knew what had happened already and made the necessary apologies and shouted at Billy in a stern voice to come downstairs and do the same. He shuffled on his feet, unable to look the officer in the eyes, not because of shame, but what he'd imagined her doing to him and herself. Bending over slightly to disguise his almost ever-present erection, he mumbled, "I'm sorry I thought you was a man" His mother's eyes bulged out as she yelled "WHAT?!" Flustered, he wondered why that wasn't a good enough reason. Billy stammered an additional, "I mean, I wouldn't have shouted it if I'd have known you were so pretty" His mother's knuckles grew white gripping the back of his chair and he stood up anticipating a crack around the side of the head.

The officer stood up and looked him in the eye, pushing her face uncomfortably close. "I don't care how attractive you think I am. You don't shout abuse at officers of the law. Do you understand?" He nodded meekly and turned as quickly as he could, almost sprinting back to his room. He could see down her top and caught a bit of top-boob and was ready to burst. His twelve-year-old brother, Damon, started to laugh at him as he bolted past. "Ha-ha! You got in trouble! Dickhead" Anger flashed through Billy as he advanced towards his sibling, intending to batter him when his mother's shriek startled him to the point of reacting like he'd been electrocuted. She was a large woman in every respect, over six-foot tall, with a backhand that could knock him to the floor. She slapped him often, and he expected one of those right now when she blocked his doorway, trembling with anger, but her words came out slow, measured and showed surprising restraint. "You're. Fucking. Grounded" Billy, too scared to argue, nodded and closed the bedroom door, locking it behind him.

Billy stayed in his room until the following morning where he was awoken by a shrill, "Billy!" coming from downstairs. He tried to ignore it, but it was followed by a more agitated "BILLY!" He knew that to be the final warning before his mother began the ascent towards him, angrier that she'd had to move than whatever irked her before. Billy sighed and yelled a response about getting dressed. He put on odd socks, since he'd used the rest of his drawer the previous evening thinking about the 'hot copper'. He gripped both rails on the stairs, inching himself down until he hovered, almost horizontal, then he pulled his legs in, swinging forward before landing at the bottom without setting foot on a single step. Impressed with himself, he sauntered into the living room to address the summons.

"I need you to go to Argos" his mother snapped, "My Elizabeth Duke necklace has come in" She thrust ten pounds and the order receipt forwards clenched in her meaty fist. "But I'm grounded!" he protested. "Think of it as a treat then!" she retorted. Billy glanced down at the money and the receipt, screwing his face up. "There's no bus fare!"

"Looks like you are walking then, doesn't it?"

"Can't Damon go?"

"He's twelve-years-old! You know he can't go to town on his own!"

"You sent me when I was twelve. What do I get for going?"

"To not have a bruise."

Her unsubtle point made, he sullenly grabbed his coat from the hook close to the rotting wooden door frame as Damon sat at the top of the stairs pointing and giggling. "You're dead" he mouthed at his brother, who responded with a middle finger and then a scramble into the safety of his own room. "Be back in an hour, you ARE still grounded" His mother gestured towards her wrist, pointing to watch that wasn't there. "Yeah. Yeah. Alright"

The walk didn't prove to be as long as he always imagined, taking only fifteen minutes. It usually seemed longer because of the route the bus took around the estate. He purchased the tacky shit from Argos and hungers pangs gnawed at his belly, so he crossed the road into Woolworths. Billy headed straight to the Pick and Mix section, that he and his friends had coined the phrase Pick and Nick, because of their propensity to steal as much confectionary as they could every visit they paid to town. The routine was simple; take the paper bag, put a few sweets in it, then pretend to be indecisive, whilst slipping one of each into your mouth whenever the security guard looked away. In reality, Billy was no criminal mastermind; the security guard earned two pounds per hour and couldn't give less of a shit about missing sweeties. He stood there as they paid him to; a walking deterrent. Billy filled his belly with sugary treats, then put the bag down and made to leave the store.

As he walked towards the exit, the security guard bolted the door. Alarmed he spun around to greeted by the sight of cashier staff closing the other exit into the shopping precinct. The guard began to walk in his direction and his eyes began to water. Billy knew they had caught him. Perhaps there had been footage of all the times he had done it before? His mum would kick the shit out of him for this, he knew it. He put his hands up and laid the groundwork for his defence, "I only had two sweets!"

The security guard passed him by, looking confused by Billy's weak outburst and began to confer with the other staff. Other customers tried to leave and sported bemused expressions on their faces. Before long, the whole store was rife with angry incomprehension to what was going on. People rattled the doors and yelled at the staff.

"Let us out!"

"We've got other places to go!"

"What's going on?"

"Open the fucking doors, you cunts!"

The store manager calmly strode towards a pastel coloured column and reached for the telephone. He punched digits in and began to speak into the receiver. He looked around the ceiling and gestured to another member of staff, who shook their head, hung up the phone, pressed another couple of buttons, nodded and handed the phone back to him. Then he began to speak.

"Ah. Erm. We're sorry for the inconvenience folks. We have been advised by the authorities that erm, there are, erm, lions loose in the area."

"Is this a joke?"

"No madam, this isn't a joke. They have apparently escaped from the circus."

"As in big cats?"

"Yes. Lions. Angry ones, by all accounts."

"Fuck off."

"There is no need for that kind of language sir, there are children in the store too. Please remain calm and we will open the doors when the authorities deem it safe. In the meantime, help yourselves to pick and mix, we will distribute drinks shortly."

Billy grinned as he made his way back to the sweets, the security guard's hand clamped onto his shoulder. "Let others go first son, you've already had a fair few." The mischievous grin on the guard's fact took Billy aback but comforted him at the same time. He complied and sauntered to the doors with other customers to peer through the windows. He'd never seen a lion, despite being scared that they were loose in his town, he remained thrilled at the prospect of seeing one.

Hours passed, his focus stayed primarily on the windows. He'd accepted offers of blue Panda Pops, the kind his mother usually served up with his Micro-Chips. His top lip had the familiar blue ring surrounding the philtrum after only a few gulps, he didn't notice and no-one else pointed it out. His hope of seeing a lion was diminishing, but persisted, long after everyone else had opted to find more comfortable areas to sit.

Day turned into night and it became impossible to see outside without pressing his face up to the glass pane which he did. Still, nothing. Eventually, the store manager returned to the phone and began to speak. Exasperated at his voice not being amplified, he again turned to the same member of staff, who looked annoyed and made the phone work correctly once more.

"Good news folks, we can open the doors. They have contained the lions. The final two were caught nearby, with thankfully, only one injury, apparently not serious. Have a safe journey home."

Relief washed over the store and people began to file out of the exits. Many opted for a drink to calm their nerves. Billy knew he needed to get home as soon as possible and began the trek back. During his journey, he concerned himself by doubting the store owner's word. What if the lions weren't all caught? What if one remained and still roamed the streets? He wanted to catch a glimpse of one, but not in the exposed open. Billy alternated between a run and a jog all the way home, jumping at any sound and meticulously scanning the horizon for cat shaped objects. Billy realised that many bushes in gardens had silhouettes that resembled lions. Something needed to be done about that.

Billy reached the safety of home and burst through the door, locking it behind him. He kicked off his trainers and removed the Elizabeth Duke bag from his coat. "Where. The. Fuck. Have you been?" his mum yelled as him before he entered the living room. He threw the bag to her and started to explain.

"It was scary and exciting mum! There were lions loose in town! We got locked in Woolworths for ages to keep us safe. They gave us free pick and mix. I didn't see no lions, but I looked out of the window all night!" With surprising speed, his mother's hand rattled his skull with an open-handed slap. Then she followed with many rage filled blows, causing Billy to turtle up on the floor and wait for it to subside. His mother bellowing in his ears, "You lying little shit! You piss off for hours, come back with blue pop round your mouth taking shit about lions! You think I'm fucking stupid? You're grounded for the rest of the year you little prick!"

From the corner of his eye, he spotted Damon chuckling. When this onslaught was over, Damon would get worse, you could count on it.

iii.

G riff was four hours into what he envisioned being a weekend long bender. He'd been drinking mainly lager, but his last order included a chaser too, setting him up nicely for the evening. He propped up the bar in the Palace Buffet; a no frills pub offering little other than seating and alcoholic beverages. Griff enjoyed the bar, partly due to it being within staggering distance of his home on the West Marsh, but also because the faces in there were familiar and largely friendly.

He wouldn't be staying here for the night however, the bar stuck to the opening hours rigidly due its location being a mere stone's throw away from Grimsby police station. Griff had also been arrested for testing the stone's throw distance measurement when leaving drunk. He needed to move on to places that stayed open later. There remained two nightclubs still open in Grimsby mid-week and either would do for him.

Griff sank the whiskey shot, glad he lived his life the way he did. He never worked for over six months a year on the industrial 'shut-downs'. During that time, he would work twelve-hour days, often six days per week. He hated it at the time, but the lack of social life meant that he never spent a penny other than basic requirements like food and rent whilst working. This afforded him the rest of the year off to spend as he pleased, with the bank balance to back it up. With great pride, he looked out of the window at the Job Centre opposite, glad he never had to set foot in the place.

The manager of the Palace Buffet eyed Griff warily. He had seen this pattern many times before. Griff was a great guy to chat to early doors, but as soon as he had a skin-full, he became belligerent and most times, violent. He'd only just been given a reprieve from his last barring and judging by the rate he demolished the pints, he was on a course for his next, final, one. Dusk had fallen outside the pub and he politely prompted Griff into moving on to somewhere else. "What are your plans for tonight chief?" Griff replied, "Probably just going to go into town and go to a nightclub. Try to pull a bird, then carry on drinking back at mine through the night. Why? You want to close up early and join me?"

Griff smiled amiably enough for the manager to return the favour. "Would that I could, Griff. I'm the only person here today. Who else will tend to the needs of this crowded public house?" The manager made a sweeping gesture with his hand at the predominantly empty pub. In the corner sat two teenagers, a coke between them, noisily slurping each other's tongues in the corner, the girl frantically mashing the crotch of his jeans as though kneading bread. Old Fishy, a man whose name he didn't know supped on a stool in silence at the far corner of the bar, lost in whatever world seemed to constantly haunt his eyes. A cackled at the window table signalled the presence of the 'Slag Nannas', two women, probably only in their forties, but both with grandchildren. They didn't mind the nickname, in fact they seemed quite proud of it. Clearly, they'd had a trolley-full by this point and would leave soon to pounce upon an unfortunate drunk twenty-something.

Griff had similar plans. The familiarity of the Place Buffet proved no match for a town full of beautiful women. His gulps from the glass grew heavier, as his friend, Dommo, burst through the doors excitedly. "Some cunts let some lions loose!" As an opening conversational gambit, it was certainly intriguing, the only people not turning to pay attention were the teenage couple, the boy now struggling unsuccessfully to wedge his hand through the buttons of her shirt without undoing them. Griff said the only credulous response he could muster, "What?" Dommo pointed at a pump, annoying the manager by doing so and continued, "Lions! Escaped from the circus. People reckon some hippie let them out! Loads of people are locked in shops in town right now".

Griff didn't believe him. Dommo held a reputation as a bullshitter, he once claimed his break playing pool was so powerful he'd shattered a black ball. "Bollocks. Jesus, fucking lions? What are you like?" Dommo looked hurt and protested, "Naw, seriously! Ring the police if you don't believe me!" Griff scoffed and accepted the offer, "Tell you what, if you're telling the truth, I'll buy your drinks all night. If it isn't true, I'm going to stove your head in. Deal?" Unhappy at even the mention of violence, Dommo nodded, but this time the truth was on his side, "Of course it is true, why would I lie about this?" Griff sneered, "Why would you lie about your Dad knocking Bob Carolgees out when you were five for making his puppet dog spit on you?" Dommo remained silent, whilst the manager used the bar phone to call the local police station.

Whilst the landlord stayed on the phone for an uncomfortably long time, Dommo squirmed. Griff's last comment had got to him. He mumbled, "Well, it was a guy what LOOKED like Bob Carolgees" Griff eyes flashed in anger towards his friend, but the manager hung up the phone and looked aghast. "He's right! Four lions got out this afternoon. They've got three of them now, but it leaves one, apparently last seen near

Sainsbury's. They say to stay put until they have caught it."

The younger of the Slag Nannas put her hand to her chest and proclaimed, "But that is near here!" Griff looked at her with contempt, "Yes, we know. Why would you need to tell us that?" Turning back towards the bar, he dutifully paid for Dommo's drink, simultaneously draining his own. "Right, I'm off" Dommo looked at his compatriot, eyes wide, "You're not serious? You said you would buy my drinks for the night!" Griff laughed, "And I will. But you'll have to be with me to get them. I was gonna leave when you came in" Domo glumly considered his options, he only had money for one drink, anyway. He turned to the manager who shrugged and nodded in agreement. Dommo decided, because of a prowling lion, to stay. He tried to salvage the prospect of a free night out.

"But what about the lion?"

"You think Griff, from the Marsh, is shitting it from a pussycat?

Griff chuckled at his own wit, and gestured Dommo towards the exit, who sulkily shook his head. Griff then exited the pub, secretly hoping he wouldn't encounter a lion on his way to town. As

74

he stepped onto the pavement, a shriek from one of the Slag Nannas alerted him to their frantic banging on the window. He pivoted and noticed two things. Firstly, all the patrons of the pub, including the amorous teenagers, gathered around the window. Secondly a huge lion turned the corner, its mane matted with what he hoped wasn't, but definitely was, blood. He'd never seen a lion. Hell, that's a reason he stayed in Grimsby, so this type of scenario never happened. Griff shook with intimidation at its size. Even on all fours, the lion stood almost the same height as him and Griff wasn't a small guy.

The lion growled, baring its fangs and fear shook Griff from his trance-like state. He didn't think he could make it back indoors without letting it indoors too and being attacked from behind. He couldn't run and there was nowhere to hide. The Slag Nannas were watching, he couldn't look like a coward. Griff did the one thing that years of hardened bar brawling instinctually told him to do; he punched the lion. He swung an overhand right straight into the side of the lion's face. Bingo! The lion recoiled and snorted, shaking its head and pawing at its face.

"Didn't like that did ya!" Griff roared at the beast, checking the window to soak in the impressed and horrified faces of the Palace Buffet clientele. His head turned for a split second, but that was all the time it took for the lion to pounce. It knocked him over, front paws landing on his chest as he stumbled backwards. Griff's ribs cracked under the weight and it dazed him after his head forcefully bounced off the concrete. He smelled the lion's rancid breath as it moved its jaws closer for the kill. Griff pushed with all his might, adrenaline coursing through his veins, he held the head and fangs away from causing any harm. The lion's claws dug in, but thankfully did not pierce his thick leather jacket. He kicked out wildly, hoping to connect with what he hoped were some testicles to send it recoiling, but dazed and disorientated, he couldn't find them.

Strength slowly sapped from his body as he grew tired. The lion proved too strong for him. He knew he would die; solely down to the fault of his own bravado. He still tried to fight, but every second that passed by meant the giant slavering head inched closer to his own. A bright light filled his vision; he knew the end had come.

Fortunately for Griff, the lights were not of some cosmic afterlife, but those of a panda car from the station opposite driving at speed towards him. The brakes screeched, and the bumper collided with the flank of the lion, sending it crashing against the wall. Exhausted, Griff lay back, not even considering what would have happened had the car not braked in time. The lion began to slope away, but as if by some final insult, stepped on Griff's groin as it limped away around the corner heading towards the Humber River.

Ribs aching, curled in the foetal position, trying not to vomit and massaging his groin in an entirely unpleasant way, Griff could only hope the lion hadn't torn his sac. He sensed the car door open and despite the blinding headlights, an officer was visible in the background.

"Sir, are you alright? Do you have any injuries?"

"What's it fucking well look like? I've been attacked by a lion, then kicked in the bollocks by it!"

"Sir, calm down, I need to check you for injuries."

Griff allowed the police officer closer to check on him. The sirens of an ambulance in the distance grew louder as it approached. Griff gradually regained his composure, noticing that the officer checking him was a woman with short blonde hair and, to him, she appeared the most beautiful sight he'd ever seen. The headlights still shone and illuminated her hair, making it almost translucent. As she checked him for wounds, Griff stated, "You look like an angel" She smiled and continued her first aid procedures, he continued, "You saved my life. Literally. Can I buy you a drink?" She laughed and replied, "I think you need to go to the hospital first. But another time?" Griff smiled. Perhaps this wasn't the worst thing that had ever happened.

The officer sighed as the ambulance arrived, loaded Griff up, who waved as the doors closed. She waved in response. It had been a long and tiring day, one that she never would have expected to be dealing with. Hours upon hours of contacting businesses telling them to close up, to keep staff and customers safe. Patrolling in the car for sightings. They had killed, thankfully, only one person, this could have been a lot worse.

She couldn't wait to get home to tell her crusty brother Charlie about this. He always banged on about animal rights, but after today's events, those cages proved the best thing for them. She reported back to headquarters over the radio to update them on the situation and where the lion headed.

"10-4. We have had reports that we have neutralised the lion. Over."

"Neutralised? Over."

"Well, they shot it. Over."

"Is it dead? Over."

"Yes. Over."

"It's sad but necessary. Over."

"Indeed. Just been told, can you come back in ASAP? Super needs a word. Over."

"Sure thing. Two minutes. Over and out."

She wondered what the Superintendent wanted to talk to her about. It was rare for the higher ups to speak to the lowly street cops individually. Perhaps to congratulate her on a good job today. 'That would be a nice change' she thought.

Black Rose.

- I'm fucking tellin' ya! I met a trainer! He said it's a dead cert!
- It's fifteen to one you doss cunt! It's a fucking nag!
- Well, I'm slamming a ton on it. Don't come crying to me when I'm minted.

Steve and Trev argued about the prospect of a bet on a horse race. Steve's insistence on the winning potential irked Trev. He considered Steve to be a born loser. Gambling wasn't his forte, nor should it be. He always lost, no matter what. His beaming face emerging with his so-called 'insider knowledge'; just another in a long line of doomed endeavours on his part.

Trev lit a cigarette as Steve bounded through the doors of the local bookmakers. He'd usually accompany him, but this time felt he needed to make a stand, no matter how minor. It was chilly outside, he hunched his shoulders, now regretting his lack of solidarity. He peered through the visible parts of the window, regarding Steve as he informed the counter woman of the bet. Trev was sure she rolled her eyes at his enthusiasm.

Neither liked the idea of viewing the race at the bookies. There hung an air of sad desperation in those places. And the faintest whiff of old nicotine. Despite Trev's reservations, he'd allowed Steve to come to his to watch the race, being that he was the one with the paid cable subscription. They walked down the road together; Steve gabbling on, spending his winnings already. Trev, largely ignoring him, wrestling with the decision to light another cigarette so soon after the last one. His boredom at Steve's droning about the horse decided for him. Only three left after this one. Bastard.

They arrived at Trev's flat, Steve plonking himself on the couch, excitedly changing the channels to find which one would broadcast the race. Trev, ever the congenial host, brought through a can of Carling for Steve and a Desperado for him. Other visitors had left the Carling at a party last month. Best way to get rid of the shit was pawn it off on Steve. Steve only noticed a friendly gesture and smiled in thanks, devouring almost half the can in one gulp.

-    More where that came from, mate.

Steve's childlike grin reminded Trev why he still hung around with him. He was a good guy, appreciated his friends and would do anything for them, other than act responsibly with his own money. More often than not, Trev, and others, would have to pay for meals or nights out to keep Steve included. Suddenly, Steve frantically waved his hands, directing Trev's attention to the screen.

- It's starting! On the TV! Come onnnnn Black Rose!

Curiosity forced Trev to watch the spectacle unfold. And unfold it did. Straight out of the gate, Steve's chosen stallion, Black Rose, streaked ahead of the competition. As the seconds passed, its lead grew, hundreds of yards between him and the rest of the field. Steve's joyous gaze flicked from the screen to Trev and back. It was hard not to get caught up with his excitement. Trev considered, perhaps his luck had changed, at least for today.

Then it happened. At a jump on the final furlong, Black Rose caught its foreleg on a hedge of what should have been a relatively easy jump. The horse pitched forward, sending the jockey headfirst to the ground, landing on his neck. Even as the camera pulled away quickly, it was easy to deduce that the Jockeys head was no longer in the forward facing position it was supposed to be. The horse landed on its legs, bucking wildly and whinnying in pain at the same time. The camera continued following the race, but Trev noted from a wide-angle shot, the horse covered quickly with a tarpaulin, a distraught trainer, holding a gun by his side. Steve's eyes brimmed with tears and Trev burst into peals of laughter.

- What the fuck! It's not funny man! Hundred quid!
- Haha... Sorry... Haha... Hahaha. You've got to see this a sign, surely?
- What do you mean?
- You place a big bet and the jockey dies, then the horse gets shot! Ha haha. See it from my point of view. You'd piss yourself.

Steve couldn't appreciate the funny side at that moment. He needed to mitigate his losses.

- I need to go back to the bookies. Put two hundred on a favourite. Get my money back at least.
- Mate, you're a fucking mess.
- Can you sub us two hundred?

Trev sighed. It was an imposition, sure, but at least Steve always paid the money back on time. He'd go via a cash machine. It was worth it to see the look on his face again.

An Accident.

Bertram Phelps, the Conservative MP for High Wycombe, wandered the streets of his constituency. He considered it a ghastly place, a haven for plebs, ne'er-do-wells and foreigners. In his addresses to his voters, his contempt for their mewling pleas was never well-disguised. But he was a master orator and had convinced them he was their safest choice. A benign dictator. That was his self-image and fantasy rolled into one.

Bertram was lost. Someone had stolen his car, no doubt a tracksuit wearing prole missing more than a handful of teeth. In his car was his phone, wallet and identification, things he did not like to take with him in the hovels they called hotels around here. These cretins had sticky fingers. Bertram grimaced at the stench of cheap perfume filling his nostrils. Bertram was angry at the floozy he'd spent the last hour with. He'd instructed her to bathe beforehand, and she'd chosen to ignore his perfectly simple request. Nanny used to have a name for tarts like her—strumpets. He liked that word, so innocent, evoking images of buttered bready treats. A far cry from the carnal drubbing he usually partook in with them.

This one had been no different. As he thrusted into her, his chin jutting out in a display of faux-dominance with her ankles beside his ears, she'd allowed herself a murmur of pleasure. More than likely affected, a part of her profession's performance. His eyes bore down into her with hatred.

- I demand silence, you cur!
- What?
- Shut your filthy whore mouth! This is MY time, MY money.

She'd objected, despite him paying for her company. The agency promised discretion for the wealthy clientele such as himself. He'd assumed that discretion went as far as obedience. Her insolent objection rankled him. With a huff, he pulled himself out of her, four inches dissolving into two as he unsheathed himself and threw the empty, but used, condom at her in disgust. She spat back at him, a thick wad of phlegm landing on his chest. 'Wonderful,' he thought, 'Now I will have to be checked for hepatitis! Alphabet edition.'

He'd used the sat nav on his phone to get to the hotel provided for him by the agency. After quickly dressing, he'd attempted to storm out of the room, before her demand for cash and threats of pimp-related violence halted him in his tracks. He fished the notes he'd brought in for payment and threw them on the floor, casting the hussy a withering glance before departing. Upon spotting the car that was no longer there, his insistence on not swearing put severely to the test. Furious, and slightly anxious, he began trudging in what he assumed to be the direction of the nearest police station.

His stride quickened as he walked past a children's play area, in which nestled a pack of feral hoodies. He bit his bottom lip as they yelled after him.

- Oi! Ponce! You lost or somefink?
- Is ya looking for a batty ta stab?
- Oi! Answer me dickhead!

He fixed his stare forwards. Through the god-awful terraces, he could spot his destination; the welcoming blue light of the law. A combination of the autumn night air and the patter of trainers jogging towards his destination sent a chill down his spine. His pace quickened, as did the footsteps behind. Only 100 yards to go. He sensed the youths behind him, but not gaining. The sight of the police station must be a deterrent. It must be. A cold sweat trickled from his brow as he maintained his speed, relief as he approached the door.

Panic overtook him as the door wouldn't budge as he pushed. He tried pulling the door. Still no give. Exasperated, he began pounding on the door as the youths stood metres away, peals of laughter erupting from them. Why had they not scarpered? A crackling voice emerged from the left of him.

- Can I help you?
- Yes, I need to come inside!
- Sorry, station doesn't allow members of the public on the premises.
- Why on earth not?
- Not enough staff to err...police the premises, if you'll pardon the pun.
- That's outrageous!
- Blame the Tories mate, they're the ones that cut back on police funding.
- I will have you know that is not the case, we merely diverted the funds to where they are more desperately needed. The nation is amid a financial crisis!
- 'We,'?

- I am Bertram Phelps M.P. for this town! Now allow me access to the building! My car has been stolen!
- Well, Mr Phillips, if you would like to report a crime, then you need to call 111. This isn't an emergency, so I still can't allow you access.
- But I don't have my phone!
- There's a phone box on the corner sir. Good night.

Bertram hissed as he was certain he heard a giggle as the intercom clicked off. He would find their superior and make a complaint; he would have their job. With a blazing temper, he turned around only to see the youths still lolly-gagging about. Fear made him tremble. He had to walk past them to get to the phone box. He trudged wearily to what he assumed to be certain doom. As they approached, tears filled his eyes, and he stammered;

- It was an accident! A misunderstanding! I didn't mean to!
- Wot you on about? You drive a jag, yeah?

Confused, Bertram meekly nodded.

- Yeah, I seen you. You walked the wrong way out the hotel ya nonce. It's over there.

Perhaps next time you'll listen when people talk to ya, ya snooty fucker.

The child was right. Bertram's eyes followed his pudgy, pointing finger and saw his Jaguar in the spot he'd left it in. Damn this cursed place, though Bertram, I'm never coming here again.

Bobby.

obby Mapples was a common sight in the Nag's Head in the village of Laceby. He would often stumble in, without fail, every Tuesday night, staggering from the methylated spirits pre-drinks he'd imbibed in his shed. The local kids claimed he lived in that shed, because of it looking considerably more habitable than his actual house. The kids never troubled Bobby, due to the rumours of his vast collection of firearms. This rumour also led to many adults also giving him a wide berth. More charitable types would insist he proved no harm to anyone and try to engage him in conversation, only to be treated to a series of un-intelligible growls when they approached. As a result, they left him to his own devices. This was fine by Bobby, as the only thoughts that crossed his mind were of a sexually deviant nature.

He didn't live in his shed, but his house had fallen into disrepair, largely due to him spending every spare penny on prostitutes. He got plenty of bang for his buck, however, since the areas surrounding Grimsby weren't exactly known for their high-class escorts. Again, that suited him fine, the whores were merely a receptacle for his frustrations. His dishevelled appearance, mottled beard and lack of technical know-how meant he would never succeed in the modern dating world. His only option; 'chuck his muck' up the drug-addled sex workers.

His visits to the Nag's Head were by design. Once a month, on a Tuesday, the pub had regular performances by the T Funky Fun-time Band. He frequented the venue every Tuesday to mask his true intent; to ogle the backing singer for the band. To him, she proved a vision. Unlike the toothless skanks he usually banged, she was a goddess. Long black hair cascaded over her shoulders like a waterfall, accentuating the figure-hugging dresses she would always wear. His eyes, narrowed into slits would soak in the delights of her ample breasts, he would draw a sharp intake of breath when the higher tempo numbers would play and the jiggle fuelled his fantasies, ones he would play out with a fish-smelling M-Kat addict every week without fail.

In his shed, where he spent a lot of his time, he practiced a masturbatory technique in front of a grimy mirror. He wanted to be able to bring himself off with no one noticing. Whilst erect, he would cross his legs, trapping his penis between his thighs, and with the slightest of movement, reach orgasm within minutes. Carefully noting any telltale ministrations and minimising them, he was ready. Ready to shower the inside of his pants with his sticky-white love for the goddess. Tonight, was the night. He finished off a bottle of Scotsmac and sauntered, with a sway, towards his mid-week home from home.

The T Funky Fun Time Band were scheduled for the evening and to his relief, they turned up on time. He positioned himself in a corner, greeting any friendly acknowledgement with a scowl and a grunt. He didn't want to be bothered. The opening salvo of Mustang Sally kicked in. He crossed his legs. It was time. She looked ravishing tonight, if only she knew how much he wanted her. He twitched his right leg, staring at her dress, a red one tonight, matching her lipstick. His eyes almost rolled back into his head as he felt the vinegar strokes come on way too early. Slow down, he chided himself. They are playing for an hour.

As they played, his arousal grew, and it became clear he would not last the entire set. Copious amounts of pre-cum served only to lubricate his thighs, making the experience even more pleasurable. He paused each ministration after only seconds, trying in vain to savour the moment. Short gasps escaped him; breathy pants as he desperately strived to contain his ardour. Then it happened. The band launched into Somebody to Love from the Blues Brothers. Her breasts bounced tantalisingly and he couldn't hold on any longer. Jets of cock snot spurted against his legs. An 8 -roper at least.

- OHHHHHHHH!! YAFUCKINGHOTSEXYSLAAAAAAAAAAGGGGGG!

Being a loner, Bobby never needed to control his ejaculatory outbursts. Prostitutes never objected, their dead eyes regarding him coldly waiting for the payment. He'd never given it a second thought. But with his outburst, the eyes of the entire pub regarded him coldly. The band stopped playing, staring at him in disbelief. It was at that moment, Bobby realised he'd made a bit of a faux pas. Not wanting the attention, he hastily made his way to the exit. A wet slap echoed through the silence and he looked down at what most of the onlookers already saw; a glob of warm jizz, had broken off and hit the floor. In retrospect, he thought, wearing shorts was a poor choice.

No Swearing.

A little context for this one. It was written on Bonfire night; the theme being Stuart era England. In the writing group, I've garnered a bit of a reputation for my foul mouth, so thought I'd play on that a little.

He sat in the tavern, drinking alone again. People gave him a wide berth on most days. He'd a tendency to babble incoherently to himself, as if in conversation with a party of others. The patrons were thin on the ground on this autumn eve, causing a furrowed brow of frustration on the burly tavern-master. Candles flickered and spluttered in the draughty drinking establishment, illuminating the face of the man as he grimaced as if hearing something he didn't like.

His gaze was directed at his left shoulder. He shook his head in disagreement. More patrons left as the man took away the allure of a social gathering, instead painting a stark picture of alcohol and being demented having close ties. The man may or may not have been mad, for what he saw on his left shoulder was a grotesque image. A squat, crimson gargoyle with black horns, unsymmetrically positioned on either side of its head. Tiny, leathery, useless wings flapped on its back. It danced around, animated as it spoke, pendulous penis flapping against its meaty thighs with a foreskin that was twice the length sashaying like a flag in the wind.

It wasn't the sight of a naked creature on his shoulder that concerned the man. He was used to that by now; he saw it all the time. The things it said often disturbed him. It often begged, cajoled and encouraged him to perform acts. Unspeakable acts of deviance with man, woman and beast. To speak ill at inappropriate times. To micturate in an alley on the Sabbath. It's cackled, garbled words pressed him. It spoke in a manner he understood, yet its tone and phrasing were not of his era.

- Go on! Just shout a bad word! It will be the height of hilarity! Give us a 'c' word!

The man hissed out of the side of his mouth.

- I told you no. There is a lady present.

He raised his glass to a black-toothed strumpet sitting across the room. She flashed a smile in return, showing what remained of her rotten teeth. The creases of her cheeks burst a pustule on her face, a creamy-yellow ooze dripped onto her stained dress. The man smiled back. He'd had worse.

- Just an 'f' bomb instead! That's a fair compromise.
- The sign says no curse words!
- That's what makes it fun! What about a 'b'? No-one gets bothered by a 'b' word!
- I made an oath to Saint Matthew that I would not profane, nor use the lord's name in vain. I walk a different path.
- If you don't, I will play with myself on your shoulder for a week.

The man sighed. He believed the creature. Why did he listen to it? He drew in a breath. Anything to close its contemptible mouth.

- F... ow!

His head jerked violently to the side as he felt a tug on his moustache from the right-hand side. His focus shifted to the heavenly creature sitting on his right shoulder. Pristine, flowing white robes billowed around the form of the most beautiful woman he'd ever seen. She demanded little of his attention, allowing him to make most of his decisions himself. He tried to avoid her serene image most of the time. It caused an ache, a longing within himself. He was ashamed there had been times he'd longingly watched her. Pleasuring himself to the sight of her ankles. He would plead with her to join in, to touch him as he played with himself like a bored monkey in a zoo. Her diminutive frame would make his thingy looked massive. She would drop her head, saddened by his lust, whilst the red creature roared with laughter. He hated to see that disappointment, hence his insistence on becoming a better man. She spoke, her voice causing a rush of blood to his nethers.

- Ignore the beast! You are doing so well. The promise you made to Saint Matthew is a step towards your betterment. Resist!
- But it says it is going to... do ungodly things to itself...
- Can't imagine how that would be... I mean, then don't look! Watch me instead. Bask in my love! As long as you don't try coating me in yours again!

She made sense. The man shook his head and steeled his resolve. He glared at the creature and stated his case in firm words.

I shall not bow to your temptation demon! Do what you will! I shall turn away!

- Please?

- No, vile wretch!
- Gimmee an 's'?
- No!
- A 't'?
- Nothing!

Defeated, the creature slumped onto its ample posterior. It looked down, and then sharply upwards again. An idea had occurred to it.

- You said no cursing, right?
- Correct.
- Well, if you can't entertain me that way. How about blowing up the houses of parliament instead?

The man turned his head to the beauty on his right. She shrugged her shoulders.

- Doesn't bother me.

He turned back to the gargoyle and nodded his head. The beast wrung its hands with glee.

- Mr Fawkes! You're the man!

Festive Cheer.

Also published in the anthology 'Christmas Gifts'.
Lowering the tone considerably.

Christ, I'm fucked. If you asked any sane person if they'd like to only work one day in a year, they'd shake their heads faster than a nodding dog in a car with broken suspension. But it isn't all it's cracked up to be. I mean, yeah, I get 364 days off per year, apart from those twatting leap years that rob me of a day's rest. But I need that time off, this one night's work is usually the equivalent of about twenty years. Magic and all that good stuff. I can't explain how it works, I'm not Steven Hawking. Suffice to say, I put in more graft in one night than many people do their entire lives.

In case you haven't figured it out yet, I know there are some slow fuckers out there, I'm Santa. Saint Nicholas. Jolly old Saint Nick. Right now, the only jolly thing about me is the prospect that I'm just over half-way through this sodding shift. You must pardon my language, but I'm fucked-in-half drunk from almost three quarters of a gallon of brandy. I swear a good portion of them mince pies had liquor in them too. I wish people would vary these treats up a bit. An evening of gorging on mince pies leaves me backed up for a week afterwards. Let me put it this way; I think I've an idea of how painful childbirth is.

I'm taking a wee break, so I sat on top of Trump Tower with my legs dangling over the edge, appreciating the view of New York. Suppose it's a perk of the job I get to see so much of the world once per year. In my time off, there is no travelling, I'm confined to the small, sovereign nation of Grotto. Lights flick on and off in the distance and I can make out small faces pressed against the windows hoping to catch a glimpse of me on my rounds. Good luck with that kids, on this night, I'm invisible, otherwise I'd have to stop to listen to every request, take photographs and all that other shite that delays me no end. I learned that lesson the hard way.

The air is crisp, at least up here anyway. New York smells like piss, mostly on street level. It does up here too, but that's because I pissed up here. I rarely urinate outside, I'm not an animal. But it's Trump Tower, and, Y'know, fuck that guy. Wearily, I stagger to my feet and command the reindeer to drop their foul payload atop the building too. I'm sniggering at how juvenile and petty I can be. Maybe it's the brandy. I flop into the sleigh and shout "Onwards Dancer! Onwards Prancer! Onwards..." Bollocks. I've forgotten their names again. "Just go, all of you!" One of them turns at looks at me with disdain. Aye, keep that up and I'll turn you into venison you red-nosed bastard!

So, I steam through most of the night, uneventfully. There's less to do nowadays, kids are way too cynical these days. They just ask their parents for stuff. Suits me fine, it's not like I get paid for this anyway, not counting all the sickly sweet confectionary and booze. It's no wonder I'm so fat. Every year, I vow to exercise and use the cross fit trainer for ten minutes a day for a week, tops. Not this year though, I'll stick to it. Deffo. Anyway, soon my evening's toil will end, but I'm facing a new problem.

This isn't a one-man operation, far from it. There're the elves. Hardworking, diligent, efficient, but a tad simple. They work the entire year, unlike me. They seem happy with having food and a roof over their heads. It's not slavery... well, it sort of is, but they are free to leave if they like. I'm sure the pointy-eared little cretins could find gainful employment in panto's and shopping malls, but they are kind of insular. They like to keep to their own. Shit, I'm sounding like a bloody racist. I'm not. It's just how they are. The elves.

There's a flip side to their work ethic. Christmas Eve comes, and they get two weeks off (I'm not a monster). These little fuckers LOVE a piss up. Whilst I'm out distributing the fruits of their labours, they are drinking almost a lake-full of berry wine. Have you ever been confronted by an army of pissed-up, leery little elves? It's an experience. I guarantee at least five of them will say they quit and call me a fat fascist. I've just got to take it on the chin, let them blow off steam. If I retaliate, then I'd have an uprising on my hands. Bugger, I'm sounding like a deep-south plantation owner again. I'm not like that!

Every year; the same situation. Whilst I'm out delivering gifts harder than a piece-work driver, those little buggers are becoming raucously belligerent. A mini riot sparks off in the workshop most years as they squabble over this and that. Their tiny fists fly towards each other with malice. And let's face it, they are three-foot-tall each, they have very little power behind each blow. They get knackered far before anyone gets more than a scrape or a bruise. Whilst their squeaky voices are squawking threats and proclamations of hate, none of the dense bastards ever think to use the woodworking tools lying about. Told you they were simple. A chisel will have your ear off if you use the fucker right.

That isn't the worst part. And remember while all this shit is going on, I'm trying to get some fucking kip after work too. The violence ends and they carry on drinking. The next stage is the make-up sing song. Tuneless fucking dirges, like a bunch of strangled rodents. If you played an Alvin and the Chipmunks LP and flicked the speeds rapidly–you'd get the idea. It's awful and led me to an attempt to soundproof the workshop two decades ago. Not only did it do very little to help, but the foam is very absorbent and the third stage of their celebrations doesn't lend itself well to the walls being covered with that type of material.

The more astute among you might have guessed what that third stage is. What do most couple do after they make-up? Yep. Angry, violent sex. Hatefucking I believe is the parlance of our times. They get the horn, big time. It's like a klaxon sounds in all their dopey little heads and they just drop their clothes and start banging. The ratio of male and female elves is skewed in favour of the males, so, well, they're forced to share. Doesn't seem to bother the Elve-ettes. They lay on their backs, all holes filled with hard Elven cock, with looks of joy in their eyes as they squeak with pleasure. A cacophony of Elf orgasms is an even more torturous sound than their frigging singing. This orgy last three days as they mix and match partners, like a coke-fuelled wife swap party.

Naturally, the party ends and as my hangover fades, theirs begins. They can't even look at each other for a few days afterwards–and rightly so. Dirty little fuckers. The entire workshop is awash with Elf sexual fluids. It smells like a shrimp factory, or worse, certain districts of London. This is where I am forced to crack the whip. That was a poor choice of phrasing, they are not slaves! But I have to make them clean up the milm and jism coating the floors, walls and crevices of the workshop. Therefore, I soon ripped out the soundproofing foam. Ever wondered why stocks in Air Wick rise in January? The place stinks. We go through a gross of those canisters, plug-ins and the likes to get the building smelling habitable again.

I'm shuddering at the prospect of it again. Perhaps this year I will film it? There must be a market for it somewhere. Worth a thought, I might be able to retire.

Bad Fan Fiction: Antiques Roadshow.

The queues gathered outside the church hall in Maidstone, Kent for the Antiques Roadshow visit to open its doors. Never had so much grey been seen in one area since the last Status Quo reunion tour. It was a warm day in April, so the queue of middle-Englanders stood in high spirits, speculating with excitement about the estimated value of the goods they'd taken with them to be appraised.

Charles Barrington-Smythe peered through the window with nervous excitement. The producers of the show, after a few years of him working behind the scenes, had been impressed with his eccentric nature and ran with him as a co-host and resident catch-all expert to be highlighted predominantly through the programme. He'd been working towards this day for a long time, but he knew something the producers didn't. He was a fraud. A trickster. A con artist. A bullshitter.

He'd realised many years ago that to add any weight to a statement, no matter how preposterous, all one had to do; speak in a plummy British accent and most would pay attention. A fake air of wealth and entitlement seemed to turn heads, and he'd turned plenty. He stood six foot tall, slender, but with a well-fed paunch. He'd recently turned fifty and didn't look a day over fifty-nine. Wire-framed spectacles, wrapped snug around his oversized head. Black hair, mottled with grey, gelled to perfection with a classic side parting. His jacket today had leather patches on the elbows to further add to the out of touch upper middle-class vibe.

He watched as the female presenter, he could never remember her name for the life of him, recorded her introduction. He remembered the celebratory party that had been held announcing his appointment. She'd explained to him later in the evening, in a drunken stupor, that she admired his 'quirkiness'. Little knowing that quirk was down to him being a working class man from Hull, pretending to be minor nobility. She was what the BBC described as 'elderly crumpet', attractive for a woman in her forties, but being the right type of screen-friendly frumpy that a show like this needed. She needed to seem both attainable and unattainable at the same time, too young for the core demographic, but easier to fantasise about than a pert twenty something.

Their conversation became flirtatious and very soon he took her in the back office, both literally and figuratively.

He winked at her from across the room and she stumbled her lines and exasperatedly waved her hand signalling to the crew she needed to start again. She stole an angry glance in return to him and he laughed back. Today was all about him.

- Positions people!

The irritatingly chipper runner had been given the opportunity to say the magic words, beaming at the chance to utter those words, almost compensating from the previous two years of minimum wage work bestowed upon him after completing his master's degree in Media Studies. Charles contemplated demanding a coffee, but he decided against it. There was time for abusing runners later. The show was about to begin. The doors opened and the jubilant throngs gathered inside the damp smelling church hall filtering to the tables clearly marked according to what type of bric-à-brac they had found. Producers pulled people out of line with what they considered were the more interesting pieces and lined them up for his 'expert' table. As they piled through the doors, he thought to himself, 'this looks like one of those

Black Friday videos in slow motion'. He smiled to himself and kept the smile on his face to affect warmth to the approaching hopefuls. Charles put in the earpiece for the producers to keep in contact with him and prepared himself to pretend he knew anything about antiques.

He'd a simple tactic to do this, since most people were looking for confirmation of what they already guessed, he merely repeated back to them what they had already told him, but in a far more verbose manner, occasionally adding in 'facts' about their origins. He sometimes inflated the prices they had suggested they were worth for a great reaction shot. Charles justified this in that by the time the programme aired, vendors would inflate their prices according to what the 'expert' had said. If they ever caught him out, he'd simply record a sincere apology and claim to have made a 'mistake'. It was a win-win as far as he was concerned.

He grew bored, the line seemed endless. As he looked down it, attempting to count how many people were in it, he spotted her. She was an example of why he wanted to do this in the first place. Charles loved older women. Much older. Producers were aware of this fact but had put it down to yet another eccentricity. Top brass at the BBC were understandably anxious after Operation Yewtree, but less fearful of a potential Operation Dutch Elm Tree. They ignored his old lady proclivities and simply never mentioned it. Charles was aware of it too. He crossed his legs as he became more and more aroused by the sight of this woman he began viewing as a goddess. Her hair was long, drenched in blue rinse. She was wearing too much make up. The sign of early stages of cataracts, milky eyes always stirred his loins deliciously. She smiled at him, showing pristine white teeth, blatantly false. 'Jackpot!' thought Charles with glee.

He dealt with the others in the line as briskly as possible; agreeing with each speculation about the value of their wares and saying he had nothing to add, other than they were from 'unremarkable times'. The producers hissed in his ear to try to make more of an effort. He ignored them, awaiting the arrival of his angel, erection not subsiding for one moment. Eventually, she arrived accompanied by a stale urine smell that stung his nostrils. He sensed an air of 'flightiness' about her and he almost stammered out a greeting.

-    Ch-Charles Barrington-Smythe. Charmed to meet you madam.

- Hello dear, my name is Rose. But you can call me Rosie.

'Right on the money there, old chap, this one's a banger!' he cackled internally to himself. He narrowed his eyes seductively and shook her hand in a deft motion; groin twinging as he felt the dry, but soft flesh of her fingers. Charles admired the relatively unblemished skin of her arms. He didn't like liver spots, but they came with the territory. He was glad to note she had very few.

- It is a delight to meet you! Have you taken the day off work today?
- Ooh bless you, I retired long ago. I found this in my attic the other day, the WI said it might be worth something. Can you tell me if it is?
- Anything for you my dear.

He gave her a wink, his trademark for many years, to which Rose giggled in response and blushed. At least he thought she blushed; it could have been rouge. He deliberated over the musty vase turning it over a few times. He noted the stamp on the bottom, faded but still slightly visible that read 'Royal Doulton, 1983' Even he knew this was worthless, he feigned astonishment as the producers gleefully encouraged him to break the bad news, content they had some great footage, despite his creepy overtures towards her they'd fix in the edit.

- So, is it worth anything?
- Rose, my word it is... it is...
- What?
- It is... priceless. I suspect the piece needs more appraisal in a private room. Gerald? Would you hold the line for a while, whilst I take Rose here to the back to give her a private consultation?
- Charles, what the fuck are you doing? That is a piece of shit! Get back on with the show now!

Charles extended his hand to lead Rose into the back room, which she accepted with a vigour of someone many years younger. He yanked his earpiece out and placed it on the table. A tinny voice was heard yelling through the speaker.

- Get the camera off him for Christ's sake, he has a visible erection!

Charles closed the door behind them and sat Rose down next to a table in a room they had designated for the appraisal of high value pieces, to be recorded for extra dramatic effect later. The camera was present, but the operator was not. Charles locked the door and pulled a chair close to Rose. He took the worthless vase from her hands and placed it on the table next to them. He grabbed her hands in his and looked her fiercely in the eyes.

- You're a very attractive woman Rose.
- Oh stop, I'm old. You don't have to flatter me you know.

He guided her hand towards his member which twitched in anticipation. As soon as her hand touched it, she pulled her hand away with a speed that surprised him for such an old woman.

- What are you doing?
- C'mon, when was the last time you touched one?
- What business is that of yours?
- I sensed you were flirting with me outside. Go on, take your teeth out and put it in your mouth.
- I will do no such thing. Give me back my vase and I want to leave.
- Fine take it. Worth fuck all anyway. Go on. Fuck off.

Rose indignantly snatched the vase from the table and shuffled away as Charles composed himself, preparing to tell people she'd responded badly to being told it was worth nothing. If he hinted towards an air of poverty and desperation about her, the rest would lap it up. He unlocked the door and allowed Rose to shuffle with indignant rage from the room. As the doors open, some of the production crew were looking at him aghast. Confused he picked up the earpiece and placed it back in his ear.

- Camera was on in there Charles.
- Shit. I'm fired, aren't I?
- Yes Charles. Yes, you are.

January 1980.

Stacey stood in the kitchen balancing a variety of chores. Whilst the washing machine was on spin cycle, she washed up and cleaned the surfaces of the kitchen. She kept a watchful eye on her son Davie in the room next door, playing Buckaroo and giggling every time the horse eventually shrugged off the plastic items. He'd requested that 'mummy play' with him, but she couldn't handle the game itself. When she tried playing it with him, her chest constricted as she trembled. The first time the horse bucked on the Christmas day, it rattled her so bad, she'd hurried off to the toilet to hide the tears that the panic caused.

Her husband, Steve, was at work. She felt awful that Davie had no-one to play with and once she'd finished cleaning, she would pull out a less stressful game or a book to spend more time with him. As if aware of her thoughts, Davie turned round and smiled at her, which she returned. The sun shone through the small window in the living room of their terraced house. The rays beamed onto Davie's head, highlighting the tight blonde curls and making them luminescent. He looked like an angel.

'Heart of Glass' by Blondie rang out from the record player she loved. Her friends extolled the virtues of the cassette tape, but she'd stuck with her trusty device. She would stack her singles up on the spindle and one would drop as soon as another finished. She didn't want a tape dictating what music she listened to in what order. Davie shuffled around on his backside in time to the music occasionally turning back towards her for approval. She again smiled back and returned a little mimicked dance of her own as she sped up the house-work to pay him more attention.

As she placed the crockery back into its assigned places, she noticed Davie had stopped dancing and now stood up, looking around the room with awe. She strained her neck to observe what he looked at, wondering if a bird had flown in. She saw nothing, but Davie appeared intent, checking every wall and corner for something she was unable to perceive. Eventually his eyes rested on her. His eyes filled with tears, but he didn't make a sound. Usually if he was upset, he would bawl in an unselfconscious manner. He seemed embarrassed and turned away wiping his eyes. She approached as she noticed his tiny fists clenching. She reached him and put her arms round him.

- What's wrong Davie?

She sensed him tense as she wrapped her arms around him and his body racked with silent sobs as she squeezed tighter. She stroked his head, trying to reassure him as he almost fought to get away. After what seemed like minutes, but merely seconds, he wrapped his arms around her as well. He didn't say a word or make a noise and her t-shirt grew sodden with his tears. Almost crying herself she repeated her question in a softer, calming tone.

- What's wrong, kidda?

Davie having seemingly regained his composure, wiped his eyes on his sleeve. He flashed a weak smile back.

- Nothing that a cup of tea can't fix.

Stacey looked shocked. He sounded like his father.

- Davie, you know you can't have tea or coffee, you're only four. Would you like a juice?
- Oh yeah. Right. Juice is fine.

Stacey tried to compose herself. He was acting strange. She poured some Robinson's cordial into his red teddy bear mug and topped it up with water, sealing it in with the lid containing the flat plastic teat that allowed him to drink from it. She boiled the kettle for herself and returned to the living room, watching Davie glancing around the room again, it was almost as if he'd not been here before.

-    Here you go. What upset you Davie?

Davie looked almost quizzically at the doubled handled teddy bear mug and grinned a little. He took a sip and placed the mug down on the table as he continued to peruse the room. He'd stopped crying, but looked sad, although he appeared to be trying to hide it, his face betrayed the fact; something was wrong.

-    Thanks Mum.

Stacey's panic rose higher within her. He never called her Mum. Always mummy. Perhaps he'd heard friends at playschool calling their mothers the same thing. Compared to this helpless feeling, Buckaroo was something she perhaps could brave for a chance to find out what was going on.

-    Do you want me to play Buckaroo with you now Davie? Come on, sit down.

- I'm all right thanks Mum. We got a pen around?
- A pen?
- Yeah. A pen and a bit of paper.
- You want to do some drawing?
- No. I need to write something down before I forget.

Curiosity overtook her concern as Stacey reached into the drawers for a pen and one of her old exercise books. B. A. Robertson's 'Bang Bang' came onto the record player. She turned the volume down a little as she remained focussed on the bizarre actions of her son. He struggled to grip the pen, trying to use it as she would, but realising that he needed to grip it using his entire fist. He then wrote, surprisingly neatly, a series of numbers separated as if a sequence. One looked like a date, but she wasn't sure.

- What is this Davie? You trying to do sums?
- No. I need you to keep this. For a long time.
- How long?
- Decades.
- What?

Concern gripped her again. She wondered if Davie was one of the idiot savants she'd read about in Reader's Digest. They were supposed to be gifted with numbers, but basically, mad. Her eyes welled up again as she contemplated how she would go about raising a crazy kid. She grabbed him and hugged him again. She'd no idea what to do.

- Davie, I'll look after you. Whatever it takes, I promise.

Davie looked like tears were about to flood from his own eyes again, but his little face scrunched in concentration and he put his hand on his mother's arm as if to reassure her. A gesture that seemed strange from a little boy, but effective nonetheless.

- I can't explain. You need to hang on to those numbers. I can't say what they are for, but you will figure it out in time. You can tell Dad, but no-one else.
- Why can't you say what they are?

He paused for a while. He seemed to struggle for an answer.

- The butterfly effect.
- What?
- The explanation is something that will also make sense later. We can forget these few minutes in time, but saying too much can't be undone.

- Davie, where did you learn to talk like this?

He shrugged.

- TV? It isn't important. What is important is those numbers. They will have such a part to play later. Please, don't forget them. Keep them safe.
- Ok I will.

Stacey had no choice but to agree. Davie smiled a sad smile to her and sat down with his juice. They sat in silence, save for the music still playing on the turntable. He listened calmly. Stacey sat next to him, stroking his curls, lost in thought about what was happening. The record player eventually went through the singles she'd organised and fell silent as well.

Davie seemed content until suddenly he looked alarmed and began to sob.

- Not yet. Just a little more time!
- What is it Davie? What's wrong?

Pain etched on his tiny face he stared back into Stacey's eyes.

- I love you Mum.
- I love you too Davie!

He wiped his eyes and held her gaze for a few seconds before his face screwed up and his eyes closed tightly and he shivered. She clasped him close, chest heaving with cries of her own. Helplessness overwhelmed her and Stacey's mind was frantic as she puzzled over what to do. The shivering stopped and through her own gasps of frustrated sobbing, Davie wailed.

- Mummy!

Davie unscrewed his eyes. Unable to view anything around him other than shadows. His mind was flooding with changes. The salty film covering his eyes not letting up, disorienting him. A cluster headache seemed to explode inside his head, causing him to stagger a little. He gripped the side of his head, the prickly stubble along the sides where he'd shorn most of his hair chafing his hands. His fingers reached the top of his head where a small area of short tight curls remained.

Images of the post diagnosis conversation remained in his mind, but the bitter recriminations of not being able to afford treatment overseas faded, being replaced by the timely windfall. He remembered the understanding smile of his mother as the results came in, the piece of paper kept for so long crumpled and disposed of without a word. His spirits lifted as he remembered the family taking a journey they'd never taken before. The treatment beginning and the hope replacing the fatalistic waiting he'd grown too familiar with.

His memories soured as it became clear it was all for nothing. The treatment was a failure and the hope he'd built in an instant was cruelly dashed as the family returned home, perhaps less prepared for what came next than they originally were. He'd not only changed nothing, but in a real sense, made it more painful for everyone concerned by instilling that false hope.

The final day he spent with his mother changed. No longer a silence as he watched her fade, unable to say anything, despite wanting to. This time she looked at him, smiling. She held his hand and told him she understood now what had happened. They exchanged mutual words of love as they'd done on that confusing day thirty-five years earlier.

The cluster headache faded, and Davie focused on his surroundings. He was still here. His sister grabbed his arm as if to steady him, both wearing sunglasses despite the grey and overcast weather. A sea of black garb. A casket with a wreath saying 'Mum'. The event he'd desperately tried to change to no avail. He wanted to go back; to figure if there was anything else at all he could do other than what he'd already tried. He would live his entire life again as a child if need be.

Davie scrunched his eyes and tried to go back. He screwed them again and again. He would settle for five more minutes. They never came.

Leaving.

Matt jolted backwards as the plane hurtled down the runway. No matter how many times he flew, he never got used to the initial burst of speed launching the vehicle into the sky. Once the shaking finished, he began to relax. They'd given him a window seat, something he didn't like as it meant disturbing people next to him throughout the journey to use the toilet which for some reason, he required more frequently on a flight.

He watched as the ground below grew smaller until clouds eventually replaced it. Matt was leaving for good. He sold off most of his belongings and now prepared for a new life. 'Good riddance UK' - his initial thought on the matter. He felt driven out by the bitterness and spite that seemed to surround him in the small town that once he called home. Now there grew a distance between him and the place he'd lived for most of his life, he wondered if it truly was the right decision.

Memories of all the good times he spent there flooded through his mind. It seemed easy to focus on the negatives, but he'd so many good friends that professed that they would miss him after he'd gone. All the laughter, all the parties and the ability to be 'known' in most of his haunts. All of that now gone, he attempted to focus on the backstabbers, on all the negative shit he could muster, but that was now already behind him. His only focus at that moment; the potential loss.

The plane's interior suddenly went dark. He assumed that being a long-haul flight, they turned the lights off to allow people to adjust to time zones. For a few minutes, he remained gazing out of the porthole style window. His eyes strayed to the tiny screen in the back of the seat. White noise static greeted him. He checked the seats adjacent; theirs' were the same. Only at that point did he scan his surroundings. The first thing he noticed was that every single screen in his eye-line contained the same flickering static. It illuminated all the other passengers in a translucent blue-white light. When he looked at the other passengers, he shivered. All sat rigid and upright, staring straight ahead with a blank expression. Their mouths hung open wide as if registering shock at the lack of broadcasts in front of them. He shook the passenger next to him for a response.

The passenger bucked like a rag doll as he shook him. After he'd finished, the passenger's head turned slow and deliberate to face him, mouth still agape, head hanging downwards as it turned, as if the effort of movement caused it to increase in weight. The eyes vacantly stared at Matt, causing him shudder. A milky white film covered the eyeballs, resembling the worst cataracts he imagined. The passengers arm rose, finger pointing in front of him, stopping at the height of the screen in front. Through the static, the word 'godly' appeared flickering, then faded away. The passenger resumed the same pose as the rest, leaving Matt to question what was going on. He began to struggle with his belt.

-   What's happening? Is anyone around?

He continued to pull at the clasp on the seatbelt, but not being able to gain any purchase. The loose nature of the belt meant he was able to stand at an awkward angle which he did in an attempt to use the screen light for a better look at the fault with the mechanism. As he did so, he caught a movement further down the plane close to the toilet area. He squinted through the gloom to try to ascertain what caught his eye.

-   Hello? What's going on?

A figure, shrouded in shadow, at the other end of the cabin, but moving without pace towards the light of the seats. Although unable to define any details, it was clear something appeared unnatural about the movements, a stumbling gait that seemed to cause whoever it was painful jerks in all their joints. In unison, the other passengers all raised their hands, forefingers extended toward the unseen entity.

Matt's body became rigid with terror. This was all too strange for him to deal with and he frantically tugged at the belt. He wanted to leave his seat, at the very least to find another sentient person who might explain what was going on to him. Then he saw what was coming. Lank, shoulder length, grey hair flowed from what appeared to be a man, but the hair flowed as if moving underwater. Its skin; wizened, brown and wrinkled. It looked to him as if it had been shrink-wrapped to its skeleton, all moisture sucked out. The eye sockets appeared empty. Large black pools replacing where eyeballs should be. The creature also kept its mouth open, similar to the passengers, but the right side of the mouth hung down lower, like it had suffered a stroke.

It wore clothes that Matt had only seen on cereal boxes. Dusty and ancient looking Quaker attire draped loosely off the shoulders, pants ragged, tied with string at the waist which to Matt appeared to be no bigger than most people's arms. He understood the jerky movements, this thing's limbs seemed brittle and unable to support any weight. I continued to lurch forward, black nothingness staring intently back at Matt from its skull. Dust, or dirt, crumbled and fell with every creaking step it took.

Matt was yanked backwards and grimaced from a dull pain in his abdomen. The belt tightened in an instant, dragging him back down to his seated position. It didn't appear to be constrict further, but the constriction left him held firmly in place. The thing's head lowered to match his new level. Wide eyed with panic, his hands tugged at the belt in vain, kicking out his legs at the seat in front of him. He still had no clue what was happening, only that he didn't want that thing anywhere near him. As he thrashed, the passengers laughed, mirthlessly, in unison. They would halt, then begin again. Cold sweat poured from him as he continued to struggle, the presence growing ever closer.

The being stood only two seats away and began to clamber onto the tops of the chairs, steadying itself on the ceiling as it used its spindly legs, which had more length than he'd noticed, because of its hunched stagger. His arms thrashed out and tears of desperation leaked from his eyes. He considered his time had come and was angry that there were no answers why. As the thing perched directly in front of him, he stammered out pleas for his life and barely formed questions. The passengers all raised their arms in unison, pointing them upwards in 45-degree angles from their bodies. Despite his fear Matt sarcastically thought them to be dancing to a village people song and forgotten what comes next.

Spindly fingers grabbed the side of his head with surprising strength. His head, fixed in place, staring back at the desiccated flesh of the thing's face. It remained still for what seemed like an eternity; the soulless, cavernous eye sockets remaining fixed on him. As he stared into them, he viewed everything he'd done replayed in an instant. He saw his life as he had lived it, mostly positive. A calm washed over him as the visions stopped. The things mouth widened and he a stench washed over him as it grew closer. He wouldn't fight it, he wouldn't beg. He closed his eyes and waited for the end.

Seconds passed, which seemed like an eternity when waiting for death. He couldn't stop himself from opening his eyes again. He blearily made out dim lights in the cabin, screens showing the flight path. The passengers were lowering their arms looking at each other with puzzled mirth. The thing had gone. He didn't know why it appeared, or why it left, but the sense of relief was a better feeling than any night out he ever had.

He could see land in the distance, the sun appearing to emerge from within it. A new chapter beckoned.

Origin Story.

Jeremy threw his schoolbag against the porch-way cupboard in exasperation. Fists clenched until his knuckles were white, tears of frustration on his face borne of impotence. He shrugged off his anorak and heaved; the back was covered in globules of spit. The bigger boys, not content with their jibes of 'Jermy gaylord' and 'pissykeks jeb-end', they sought to further humiliate him by covering his back with gob. All the good things he'd ever done for people and all they remembered was that one time he'd pissed a bit when laughing at a squirrel.

'No more' Jeremy thought with a grim determination. It was time to fight back. He'd watched all his father's Bruce Lee films repeatedly, to the point where he knew the scripts and the actions off by heart. "Bullshit, Mr Han man" he barked at his reflection in the back door. The house was empty, Jeremy was a latch-key kid left to his own devices most evenings. That suited him just fine. "Want some tea?" He mimicked Bruce Lee from Enter the Dragon and slung a packet of micro-chips in the nuker.

Whilst he'd learned the moves, he'd been afraid to use them. He'd get into trouble, especially if he killed one of them by accident. He needed to be incognito; become a spectre to strike fear into their hearts. Like any self-respecting superhero, he needed an alter-ego. It was time to make a costume. He stomped up the stairs to his room, his eyes catching on his Lego Marvel collection; still boxed. 'They'd be worth some money one day,' he told himself. Inspiration struck him like a wad of phlegm on his back from the bullies. He needed to borrow his parent's clothes to complete the disguise.

Cautiously, he opened his parent's bedroom door. He'd made the mistake of bursting in there before, the memory of his mother pressing a stiletto heel into his dad's knackers sent a shudder down his spine. Satisfied they weren't in there this time, he sauntered over to their wardrobe, searching for a disguise. He found a leather mask with a zip on the mouth. Perfect! With trembling hands, he pulled it over his head. There were no holes for the eyes, this was no good. He breathed in a sigh of frustration and his nostrils filled with the stench of stale urine. "Blech!", he ripped the mask off and threw it back into the wardrobe.

After several minutes of rummaging, discarding all manner of strapped leather items, he hit pay-dirt. A black eye mask, similar to the kind Robin used to wear in the old Batman cartoons. If it worked to hide Dick Grayson's identity, it would do so for him too. A hooded cape was the next thing to fall into his excited hands, he draped it over his shoulders and practiced kung-fu in the mirror. He looked awesome! But the cape had no fastenings, he needed something to tie it, and the outfit together. He came across a thin red scarf, with a jewelled amulet fastened to the centre. He tied it around the neck of the cape, impressed with his haul.

One thing still troubled him; it still exposed his facial features. He needed further cover. His mother's make up cabinet held just the ticket. He blackened up his eyes behind the mask, adding to an air of menace he was positive he exuded. Using bright red lip gloss, he coated his mouth, chin and cheeks with the goopy red liquid. He admired himself in the mirror again, it reminded him of another time he'd barged into his parents room. His father, lay prone, head between his mother's legs, looking up in alarm when Jeremy entered. He must have done the same thing, as his father's chin looked similar. Jeremy recalled the angry shouts and murmurs about 'Aunt Flo'. To this day, he'd still never met her. His eyes blazed; He looked terrifying.

It was time to hit the streets. After his chips and blue pop. He guzzled them down as fast as he could, giving himself hiccups. He waited for them to pass. It took two hours. By the time he was satisfied the painful ministrations had stopped, it was dark outside. Just the right light for him to dispense his dark justice. He strode into the night with a purpose. Vengeance would be his. It wasn't long before the targets of his wrath came into view. They were hanging round the shops, teasing a tied up Alsatian.

"Your reckoning is nigh!" Jeremy boomed, voice cracking a little as he did so. Fear gripped his slight frame as he pumped his fists to ramp up his adrenaline. The wrong-doers now knew of his mighty presence. "What the fuck are you doing Jermbox?" Curses! One of them knew his secret identity. The four boys loomed towards him. "Behold, the magical amulet of Kuntata!" They looked confused, as rightly they should, "The amulet will befuddle your tiny little minds!". Jeremy waved his arms mystically, like Doctor Strange. They all laughed. He tried to intimidate them with his incredible martial-arts prowess.

The lads continued to laugh as Jeremy hollered whoops and clumsily kicked his legs out and flailed his arms. Infuriated by their mocking mirth, he stepped into overdrive, adding spinning attacks to his repertoire. His foot caught the edge of his cape, jerking his neck sideways and causing him to trip, landing awkwardly on the curb, his neck hitting it with a sickening crack. They continued to laugh. Jeremy looked on, unable to move, experiencing an unpleasant grinding sensation as his body spasmed on the floor. Helplessly, he watched in horror as they all doubled over, the hilarity too much for them to bear.

Then it happened. Their grey school trousers darkened as the fits of laughter caused them to empty their bladders. Demented peals becoming looks of panic as their eyes filled with tears and they turned heels and ran as Jeremy barked after them "Who's got pissy-pants now you fuckers!". Their footsteps echoed into nothingness in the night as Jeremy's eyes felt heavy. Before they closed a final time, he whispered "Victory is mine!"

A Lover's Quarrel

- I don't see what's so fucking hard about this!

Tarquin slammed the door as he exited the living room of the house he shared with Sally. He leaned against the kitchen sink, frustrated and breathing in laboured, rasping wheezes. His thoughts had become clouded with rage. He'd have never thought she was capable of such brazen disregard for his passions. Their three-year relationship now dangling by a miniscule thread because of her perceived ignorance.

He considered when they first met, the poor choice of going to the cinema, unable to communicate with words. He thought of the excitement he felt at their proximity that day; her little finger stroking the back of his hand on the armrest. By the time the film had ended, their hands became entwined and elation filled his soul, anticipating the kiss that would soon follow. After a McDonald's, obviously.

Tarquin loved Sally. Of that he was sure. With that certainty came the threat that it was perfectly feasible she didn't love him back. Today was proof of this and he choked back tears, running the tap in front of him to disguise the noise of his weakness. He had to give it one more try. He had to. Wiping his eyes, he turned off the tap and strode back to the living room.

Sally sat, arms cradling a cushion, eyes red. She'd obviously been crying. As sad as it made Tarquin to see her unhappy, it meant she still cared. As softly as he could, he sat next to her, offering a comforting arm.

- I'm sorry Sal, I do love you. You know that, right?

Her eyes flashed with anger, the venom the glare she cast made Tarquin afraid for their union once more.

- I only said I wanted to put on Days of Future Past! YOU said you wanted to watch a Marvel film! What's your fucking problem?
- Days of Future Past isn't a Marvel film! It's a Fox film, part of the X-Men franchise consisting of six main entries, three Wolverine films and, to a lesser extent, two Deadpool movies, which admittedly,

can be a part of any universe, especially now that Disney have bought Fox!
- It says Marvel at the beginning! On screen! You twat!

Tarquin choked back his rage and tried to calmly explain. Once again.

- The Marvel Cinematic Universe comprises twenty-one films, beginning in 2008 with Iron Man. It is its own entity and nothing to do with the X-Men franchise other than the source materials original publishers.
- Ok. Let's stick the Amazing Spiderman 2 on then! I haven't seen that.
- Fuck you. You know full well that isn't part of it either.
- Spiderman is.
- Only Homecoming. And Sony own that. Marvel produce it.
- What about Fantastic Four?

Tarquin wiped a tear from his eye. It seemed clear she wanted to hurt him.

- I said we don't talk about that.
- What about the old Marvel films then, Mr expert? Blade! Daredevil! Nick Fury starring David Hasselhoff!

- I've. Already. Explained this. Marvel had financial difficulties in the nineties, so sold their properties off to a variety of studios. The only ones still with rights today are Fox and Sony. They have spent ever since regaining the right to their own works. That's why it all started, finally in 2008.

Tarquin's watery eyes looked at Sally pleadingly. She maintained her steely, defiant gaze, until it cracked, her face erupting into shrill laughter. She slapped him playfully on the arm.

- Look at you, you dick! You're getting all wound up over silly films! I was winding you up! Stop crying and give me a hug.
- I'm not crying, it's dusty. And they're not silly...

Sally grabbed him, squeezing his head against her, reluctantly, he reciprocated until she exhausted her affections and sat back, remote back in hand, scrolling through Netflix. Tarquin sat, tense from the adrenaline caused by their tiff. Everything was fine again, for now. Sally hovered over a selection on the screen.

- What about Batman vs Superman?
- GET OUT OF MY HOUSE!

The Aftermath

Wood cracked and splintered as a claw hammer's prongs pulled out a nail in sharp, stiff motions. Maria, beads of perspiration on her brow, worked feverishly to remove the boards from the outside of her home in the forest. She wanted to allow natural light into the house for the first time in almost four months.

Eleven years earlier, her husband, Jonny, had spent months persuading her to look at the place it was impossible to imagine her life without. She hated the idea of living far away from people, the nearest town in their Canadian province being thirty-seven miles away. The reclusive life wasn't one she'd ever imagined for herself, but eventually she had agreed to the two-hour drive to visit and saw why he was so insistent. Lush, green trees for miles around and within a twenty-minute hike uphill, a person could see the Pacific Ocean. She'd agreed there and then. It was a decision which proved to have saved her life.

Maria, with an effort, pulled the final board from the window and cast a wistful glance at the headstone in the garden. Jonny wasn't buried here; she mixed his ashes with the soil in the property they'd shared as per his wishes. His illness was sudden and painful. Months of long stays in a hospital where Maria accompanied him; her remaining positive and stoic, whilst he pleaded with God to end the pain. On the rare occasions she wasn't by his side, she would weep for hours, huge racking sobs that made her head pound and her throat hoarse. Her strength was not enough to cure what ailed him. Despite her soothing and optimistic words, Jonny passed soon after, leaving her devastated and alone.

Jonny had little in the way of possessions, trinkets mostly, but one thing he owned that irked her was an old, thick, smelly hemp tow rope. For reasons she would never fathom, the rope held a more sentimental value to him than any other possession. When she asked him why, he'd smile and repeat the same phrase, "It's strong. Like you. Like my grandparents who bought it. Each strand coming together to form a bond, like what we have. How can I ever throw that away?" It was that rope, fashioned into a noose that hung from the thickest beam of the ceiling in the home. She'd first fashioned it this way when he'd died,

142

years prior and in her lowest points, where the grief threatened to consume her, she considered ending her own life. Maria considered the gamble that there was something after death that would reunite them. Jonny would not have wanted that outcome for her, she knew this, so she carried on, living a solitary life in the forest, with his headstone for company. Now the noose hung, swaying gently in the breeze for a different reason; it was there as a last resort.

She'd seen countless movies by hack directors over the years, a re-occurring trend generating a slew of low budget zombie movies. It was B-grade cinema at best; the stuff of nightmares for some, cynical laughter for others. Then it happened for real. The recently dead began walking, attacking other people, infecting them, spreading their disease. All speculation about what these shambling monstrosities were capable of quick to be debunked as almost half of the globe's population fell victim to them in the space of a month. Maria detested guns and refused to own one, even after a scare with a neighbouring bear caused Jonny to consider buying one out of panic. The only time she'd regretted her decision, was when she contemplated what would happen if the dead forced their way through the barricades she'd built–a quick way to prevent an agonising death. Jonny's precious rope was her 'Plan B'.

When the emergency broadcasts warned people to stay indoors, she'd used planks to secure both the inside and outside of all the breakable glass on the property. She'd left gaps, to allow scant visibility in case of a tactical exit, either from the house or her mortal coil. She'd covered the well outside too. The electric and water supplies never stopped for the entire time, but the house was more than equipped to deal with such things, as there would be times when harsh Canadian winters would freeze the pipes and cause blackouts, sometimes for weeks. They'd owned a backup generator and maintained a well as an alternative source of water. To ensure a falling corpse wouldn't taint that supply was a priority.

After securing herself indoors, she waited. The emergency broadcast on the radio became a whine of static, which she kept on the lowest volume possible permanently, replacement batteries close at hand. Because of their remote location, they stockpiled tinned food and bottled water in their cellar, accessed only from within the house. During the harsh winter months, travelling to the nearby town proved impossible, so she and Jonny quickly learned to make good use of powdered milk products, bread making machines and adjusting from a kind of living that most town and city dwellers take for granted. She knew during the outbreak she wouldn't starve.

It'd surprised Maria how easy surviving a zombie apocalypse proved to be. The most difficult part for her was pushing her giant refrigerator up the pull-down stairs to her bedroom. She kept a supply of food and water in there too, in case of being trapped at night. Maria controlled the access to the room from within, securing the steps at night, so rest would come safe knowing nothing could grab her in her sleep, although before doing so, she regressed to her six-year-old ways of checking the closet and under the bed for 'monsters'. As she'd scraped the hefty fridge to the base of the stairs and pushed, the strain causing her legs to buckle and her back to scream at her to stop, Maria had never felt more alone. After it had breached the second step, sweat pouring down her back and stinging her eyes, she'd realised there was no turning back. If she stopped, the weight of the fridge and gravity would cause her an injury before she could get out of the way. Through sheer will and exertion, she pushed the metal box each agonising step, before finally collapsing onto the floor panting, but charged with both relief and accomplishment at the Herculean task she'd completed.

Then boredom hit her. Despite still having electricity, she used it sparingly. If the backup generator came into play, it would become a finite resource, not one available for entertainment purposes. Besides, the film collection she and Jonny amassed over the years were mostly from the horror genre, hardly appropriate, given the situation. Light was scarce and served as a potential beacon to her would-be attackers, so she kept it to a minimum. Maria had always been a voracious reader throughout her life, but seldom held on to a book for longer than the time taken to read it. She'd donated most of her purchases to charity shops as an attempt to 'pay it forward'; to expect a karmic return that did not bear fruit. Her last batch of purchases read through multiple times, now irritated her, so her eyes were instead drawn to Jonny's modest collection of fantasy and sci-fi. These genres held no interest to her, but she needed to focus on something other than the isolation and the horrors lurking outside.

And lurk they did. There was no dramatic pounding and moaning at the windows as the films she'd watched suggested. Figures shuffled from within the surrounding trees, then stood still, swaying figures silhouetted by the moon at night. At first, just one stood almost motionless facing the house, eyes staring, but unfocussed. Maria's terror rose when the first of the deceased emerged, heightened when after a few days, it was joined by four more. Eventually, she saw the only threat they posed was if she left the house. After three weeks, she barely looked out of the window to check. The dim glow of her reading lamp in the bedroom and the occasional bathroom light the only things that seemingly animated them, and then only for a few seconds before they resumed their vacant gaze.

She devoured the texts of her beloved's only vice. She considered every single one trash, bored by clumsy metaphors and over-used tropes. It became a quest to see if any of the books Jonny owned proved not to be the form of fantasy obsessed with conquering and sleeping with elves, aliens and wood sprites. All seemingly sharing the same traits; huge breasts, long legs and a slight oddity—pointy ears here, green skin there. She scribbled notes; scathing critiques of the power fantasies of the authors and their gender politics. With every bilious word she wrote about the novels, Maria also found herself thankful to every tale. They were keeping her sane. Halfway through a particularly misogynistic chapter about a warrior king seducing and bedding three nymphs, the radio crackled into life. Maria bolted to turn up the volume.... ***reversed using spores. The scientists discovered they bonded with necrotic tissue, re-vitalising it. Preliminary tests have shown the affected having full cognitive function returned. A huge global effort is underway to produce large quantities of the spores, which multiply and spread from outside to within. We do not consider these spores harmful to the living, but there may be side-effects including, but not limited to, headaches, vomiting and light diarrhoea. These symptoms should not persist as the spores will die out after around seven days. Listen out for aircraft which will be spraying. Upon hearing this, it is advisable to wait seven hours before exiting your property. Message will repeat.***

Maria rushed to the window, peering through the cracks of the wooden barricades to search skywards for signs of planes. Four hours later, she heard the roaring of engines, but was unable to locate the source. Then it appeared to rain, huge blue droplets bouncing from the ground and floating, glistening in the sunlight. As if sentient, she watched amazed as the droplets rolled under the door frame, splitting and bouncing around the house. Maria laughed as they rebounded from the walls, elated by what they represented; an end to the crisis or the renewal of hope.

A cough rang out, breaking Maria's transfixed state. She rushed back to the window. She counted nine figures outside, three of which had dropped to their knees, soon followed by the rest. Looks of confusion echoed across their faces before realisation kicked in. Some cried, others smiled with joy. Their nightmare was over. Slowly, they departed the area around her house leaving Maria to her cautious optimism. She returned to the inter-species foursome.

It was two days before Maria opened her door. She waited to see if there were any reports of failure, but none came. As she embraced the warmth of the sun on her skin, waves of euphoria washed over her. She sprinted inside to get the hammer to remove the boards. Before working on the well, the noose again distracted her. Maria placed the hammer down on the well's makeshift cover and returned inside untying the knot at the base and threading it back through the beam to remove it entirely. With the rope looped around her arms, she walked to the rear of the house where beyond the fence was a steep incline lined with trees. Maria hefted the weighty twine over the fence listened to it crashing against the branches in the distance until it came to a stop. She wouldn't need it anymore.

The overwhelming urge to visit town prompted Maria to abandon the works she'd started, so she pulled her keys from a dish beside the door and slipped into her car. Maria experienced mild disappointment as the scenery was far from being the post-apocalyptic wasteland she'd expected. No plumes of smoke, no crashed cars or debris of any kind. The end of the world hadn't been as destructive as she'd expected. She experienced further shock as she arrived in town almost an hour later. Maria expected quiet, almost deserted streets as people struggled with the events of the past few months and slowly rebuilt their lives. It was the opposite, the town was a hive of activity, a jubilant atmosphere, faces wearing smiles. The buoyant sensation washed over her too and as she flitted from store to store, she found herself unusually chatty.

It was easy to spot who had been infected and recovered. Their pallor with a tint of yellow, no doubt caused by the lack of kidney function. Some had visible wounds, bite marks mostly. The spores appeared to not only cure the zombification but also the added effect that it would regenerate missing flesh, bubbling it back into place before eventually smoothing out, leaving only a discoloured patch as opposed to a scar. The victims' mouths appeared dry and cracked, another blemish that would dissolve over time as they rehydrated. Maria chatted to a store clerk, wondering why so many businesses succeeded in getting back up and running so quickly.

The clerk informed her of a nationwide understanding that businesses offered double pay to those returning to work as soon as possible. After all, how much sick time was necessary to recover from death? No-one knew. People welcomed the opportunity to return to a normal, boring working life, and the town indicated how the majority across the country and the globe dealt with the crisis. Maria exited the store, returning to the car to place her purchases in the trunk of her car, before ordering a coffee nearby to drink whilst observing the world heal from a distance.

The triumph of the human spirit amazed Maria. In face of adversity, people struggled against their weakened states as if to scream to the universe they would not cower or be beaten by something as trivial as an extinction event.

They re-doubled their efforts to experience a semblance of normalcy. It was inspiring. Maria resolved to re-visit the town far more often as the weather allowed. With the self-promise of more social activity in the future, Maria left the town and began the drive back to her home. She flicked through radio stations, some still broadcasting static, others discussing recent events. No music appeared to be playing, so Maria left the radio on a station she used to enjoy as the presenter reported the latest news.

As production of the spores continues, pharmaceutical companies enter a bidding war to control the supply for future use for what many are referring to as the literal cure for death. The organisation responsible for the breakthrough insist that it would be unethical for a company to control production solitarily and that the long-term effects are still to be determined. The spores have already disappeared, far more rapidly than anticipated. The creators state they refuse to co-operate if their parent company accepts any offer.

Maria switched off the radio. Moral debates were something she didn't want to listen to right now, and she imagined the same issue would be discussed at great length on other stations. She wanted to maintain the happy vibe for as long as she was able. She cheerfully hummed to herself as she drove upwards through the picturesque, winding roads on the hills towards home.

Maria unloaded the car, packing supplies into the cellar. As she closed the trunk, a loud 'crack' startled her as it echoed through the forest. As her panic faded, Maria realised it was a sound she'd heard many times in the past; moose aggressively locking antlers to determine who gets to sleep with the females. She gasped out a nervous laugh and returned to her previous work, removing the barricades from the well and then tackling the problem of returning the refrigerator to the kitchen without somehow allowing gravity to destroy parts of her house.

She couldn't choose which job to tackle first however and grew distracted by the memory of the popsicles she'd bought in town. The prospect of the treat proved too tempting, so she unwrapped one of the icy treats, picked up the hammer in preparation, then sat propped up against the stone wall of the well, savouring the sensation of the cold with the heat outside. She switched on the radio. Again, no music, but left it on anyway.

... harrowing. Here is the interview.

So, the question on everyone's lips is, do you remember what it was like?

Oh yeah bud. I remember everything. It was like something trapped me inside my body, eh? I wasn't in control of my movements or nothing, bud.

You were fully conscious?

Yeah. It was kind of like everything was in black and white though yeah? Apart from people. I could see them from miles around. And my body would always go to where they were. I wanted to make it stay where it was. I was real hungry, but I knew what it was my body would eat.

You attacked people?

Everyone did. That doesn't make it easier. I don't like horror movies. This was like having to watch one permanently. No looking away or hiding behind a cushion. It forced me to watch.

Maria listened intently. She tried to imagine how hard that would be, all her thoughts and feelings conflicting with her own horrific actions. The interviewees voice hushed after they asked a question about the killings. She heard a gulp and his voice trembled.

My mom. She was the first. Inside, I'm screaming and telling myself to stop. She started crying as I drifted towards her and I'm terrified for her. I wanted to tell her to run, but she looks at me, eyes full of tears and says, "I love you honey". I couldn't cry, but it's like I was. She held her arms out to me and I felt them wrap around me as my face went to her shoulder, then pull back ripping bits of her away. Mom held on to me as I got drenched in her blood, she didn't scream. She just grunted and took the pain until she slipped away. My body stopped attacking her and sort of stood around for a while. Then she got up. I wanted to say sorry. But my lips said nothing. Then we saw a person. Like through the walls or something and we walked together.

A tear streamed down Maria's face as the interviewer in a compassionate tone offered commiserations. She thought of Jonny, watching him slowly die and empathised. Surely this wasn't restricted to one person. How many others committed similar deeds?

She was shot. In the head. She didn't come back. We were going towards a guy, it happened to the side of me. I couldn't even turn to look back, my body carried on moving forward towards him. He ran away, and I didn't catch him. I wish I hadn't come back. My mom didn't.

Maria jumped as the presenter offered further condolence and a gunshot blasted out through the speakers of her radio. It cut to a different voice.

That was earlier today. Since then, we've had floods of reports of suicides coming in as people struggle to cope with their actions during the crisis. I urge anyone that is feeling this way to seek counselling wherever they can. As bad as it may hurt, you're far from alone. Please don't kill yourself.

A hand, from out of nowhere, forcefully grasped at Maria's hair, wrenching her aside as she flailed for the hammer nearby. Her fingertips grazed against the handle as the attacker stumbled, landing on top of her chest, knocking the wind out of her. She struggled to catch her breath, whilst pushing an arm up against the throat of the figure, threatening to push their face ever closer. Milk-white film covered the eyes of the assailant, masking burst blood vessels. Maria's arm chafed against the throat, or more specifically, against the rope wrapped around the neck. This person had killed themselves, using the Jonathan's rope she'd discarded.

It used to be a woman, the mottled face still streaked with mascara signifying their state of mind before they died. Maria still held the mouth at bay with her arms as it continued to press downwards, the rancid smell of decay emanating from the open mouth inches away from her face. Maria's free hand blindly reached for the nearby hammer.

It's happening again. Every person who dies is coming back. It is time to go back indoors. The spores are gone, but they didn't solve the problem; they just treated the symptom. I repeat, the recently dead are still coming back. Please, please, don't kill yourself. You will have to live through it all again and cause more people to do the same.

Maria stopped her frantic efforts to grasp the hammer, instead her hand found the rope and pulled, relieving some pressure from her opposite arm, which she quickly shifted to the shoulder, barging further weight off her own body allowing her to buck off the infected body. Scrambling to her feet, Maria sprinted around the well, still gripping tightly to the rope, tying it around a post to the ornamental roof covering the mouth.

She gasped, body still fighting to recover from the exertion and picked up the hammer, holding it in both hands pointed towards the figure straining against its bonds with an effort to reach her. Maria gulped down air, panting as she regarded the former person in front of her. The guy on the radio had said he was still 'in there'. This had been a young woman, her clothes making her look barely out of her teens. Maria stammered, "I know you can hear me. I don't know what to do! Do I run? Do I kill you? Do I lock myself away until the spores come again?" Not a flicker of a response was visible on the zombie's mottled face. The rope had grazed away the soft flesh on the neck of the girl, surrounded by purple and red bruising. Maria gripped tighter on the hammer as she backed away towards the door of her house.

As she reached the door, eyes never leaving the girl, she couldn't close it. Maria tried to imagine the despair that would cause someone so young to take their own life alone in a forest. She dropped the hammer and cried, reliving the sorrow she'd also experienced when the person meaning the most to her in life had gone. The spores would no doubt come again soon. This girl would still be in turmoil. Maria started back towards her, each step threatening to change the foolhardy decision she'd made. "We'll be back to normal soon. I'll help you through this when we get better. We're miles from anyone here. By the time we get near other people, the crop sprayers will be back. Remember, I'm letting you do this, there's no guilt to feel." Maria walked to the other side of the well and released the knot, tied only moments ago. As the girl lurched forwards, Maria opened her arms to embrace her. She was barely able to wrap them around her before teeth sank into her clavicle, her blood warming her face as they both fell to the ground.

An hour later, Maria saw the world, devoid of all colour. Her body clambered to its feet. She saw the girl at her side, then something drew both of their attention to a speck in the distance. They both shuffled together into the surrounding trees, the rope still trailing behind the tragic girl.

... *and if you truly cannot carry on. For your own sake, for everyone else's sake. Do as the person on the interview did. Shoot yourself in the head, because otherwise, you'll come back.*

Acknowledgements.

A big thank you to the writers at the Globe who meet every Tuesday. Gemma, Matthew, Mike, Andy, Rebekah, Katie, Samantha, Eve, Kate E, Victoria, Sally, Dave and Connor.

Also, big thanks as ever to my parents and brother, Andy and his wife, Kerry. I couldn't ask for a better family.

And my friends Dave H, Claire R, Nolan, Wrighty, Jimmy B Lethal, Kerry J, Nic, Vic and Rik. And Rob Mitchell, whose novels Four Seven Two and The Thirteenth Step are also available on Amazon.

There's been a lot of great support I've had over this past year, so if I have forgotten anyone, it isn't intentional. Please leave a review on Amazon if you enjoyed this, it helps out a lot.

.

Printed by Amazon Italia Logistica S.r.l.
Torrazza Piemonte (TO), Italy

10348164R00093